"GREAT GOD ALMIGHTY,
LOOK AT THAT."

A large luxurious automobile stood at the curb, a magnificently American monster, all glitter and glass. The rear wheel was flat.

O'Halloran found the key that unlocked the door of the trunk. He twisted the key and the door popped open.

"Good God!"

"No jack?"

O'Halloran pointed and the priest went out into the street to look into the trunk.

The body lay on its side, nude except for jockey shorts. The sightless eyes stared straight ahead. The flesh was eerily white. There was little doubt that the man was dead.

────────────── ★ ──────────────

"Father Dowling readers will find the contemplative parish priest...in fine form."
—*Chicago Tribune*

RALPH McINERNY

FOUR ON THE FLOOR

WORLDWIDE.

TORONTO • NEW YORK • LONDON
AMSTERDAM • PARIS • SYDNEY • HAMBURG
STOCKHOLM • ATHENS • TOKYO • MILAN
MADRID • WARSAW • BUDAPEST • AUCKLAND

For Anne and Chris Policinski

FOUR ON THE FLOOR

A Worldwide Mystery/October 1994

First published by St. Martin's Press, Incorporated.

ISBN 0-373-26154-3

CONTENTS

The Ferocious Father

A FATHER DOWLING MYSTERY NOVELLA

ONE

ROGER DOWLING sat in his rectory study with a copy of Dante's *Purgatorio* open on his lap. His eyes were closed. It was early afternoon, and he had lunched all too well after saying the noon Mass and was now engaged in unequal battle with the desire to take a nap. No doubt this was why he did not hear Marie Murkin admit his visitor nor hear them approach down the hall.

"Father Dowling," Marie said, with a burble in her voice. "This is Mr. O'Halloran."

"Good day to you, Father Dowling. Would I be disturbing you now or could you give me a bit of your valuable time?"

The man was short to the point of dwarfishness, and Roger Dowling was sure he would have been reminded of a leprechaun even if it had not been for his visitor's exaggerated brogue. Roger Dowling had met his share of professional Irishmen, usually several generations removed from the old sod yet finding in those distant origins their self-identity. Chicago, he had been told, was second only to Boston and New York in this regard.

"Now don't you be moving for me, Father," O'Halloran said, darting into the study when the priest began to get to his feet. "I won't be disturbing your rest more than need be."

Roger Dowling was aware of Marie Murkin beaming behind the intruder and was only partially reassured. If the housekeeper had any fault it was to keep visitors *from* the pastor, either presuming to advise them herself or deciding they were fakes and sending them on their way.

"You can't possibly know that, Marie," the pastor had often protested.

"Believe me, Father Dowling, after all these years I can spot them a mile off."

"Perhaps. But until you're ordained and appointed pastor of St. Hilary's, I'll be the judge of that."

"Ordained!" Marie snorted.

"You have definite signs of a vocation, Marie." If Roger Dowling had any besetting fault, it was his tendency to tease the housekeeper. In this case, he knew that those who agitated for women's ordination had no ally in Marie Murkin. There were days when he doubted whether she approved of the ordination of males to the priesthood. "Not that I think you would hear of demotion to mere pastor."

But on this occasion, it was clear that she more than approved of Michael O'Halloran.

"What a wonderful parish you have here, Father Dowling," the little man said.

"I don't often hear that."

Marie made a noise and left, and O'Halloran awarded the remark a smile.

"I'm with Dasher Development," O'Halloran announced, as if revealing his royal birth. He gave the pastor a chance to express astonished surprise, and when that did not happen, said, "Of course you've heard of us."

He did not wait for a reply to that. Roger Dowling had never heard of Dasher Development, but there seemed no charitable way to prevent that lack in his education from being corrected then and there. Had O'Halloran brought that briefcase with him into the study? The pastor had not noticed it until O'Halloran unzipped it and began to deal out brochures, pamphlets, glossy charts, graphs and columns of figures.

Dasher Development devoted itself to helping parishes, religious orders, missionary societies, and other church-related entities raise the money needed if they were to flourish. That O'Halloran had seen promise in St. Hilary's was less of a mystery now. Dowling would have stopped the man before he got going, but O'Halloran was irrepressible and it was difficult not to become fascinated by his pitch—fascinated, not tempted. In the day of the television preacher, O'Halloran's methods might seem subtle, but they were offensive enough for the pastor of St. Hilary's. The technique of fund raising seemed to depend upon and cater to the vices of potential donors. Gifts received adulatory acknowledgment, and those whose vanity proved immune were made to feel shame for their stinginess. It was O'Halloran's task to make people see that the salvation of their souls required uncalculated generosity as far as the needs of the church were concerned.

"I think of it as my ministry, Father."

"I'm not surprised."

"St. Luke was a tax collector, wasn't he?"

"I think you mean St. Matthew."

O'Halloran accepted the correction with such good grace that Roger Dowling had the feeling the mistake was intentional and he had risen to the bait. Undeniably, he felt almost protective toward O'Halloran, at least for a moment. An expression of anguish flickered on the wizened face.

"A mistake like that, Father. It destroys a whole presentation."

"St. Luke will forgive you."

"Don't you mean St. Matthew?"

Roger Dowling smiled enigmatically and O'Halloran went on.

"A tax collector is a kind of fund raiser, isn't he? I think of him as my patron. St. Matthew." He glanced at the pastor. "How many souls in the parish, Father?"

As many as there are bodies, he might have said in protection against the unction with which O'Halloran asked the question, but he did not want to sound flip or, worse, skeptical.

"Have you worked in the archdiocese before, Mr. O'Halloran?"

"Worked in the archdiocese," O'Halloran repeated and laughed tolerantly. "Is the Pope Polish? Do you know Bishop Larson?"

"We were classmates."

"Aha." O'Halloran's darting eyes seemed to discard one approach and select another. "What we do, Father, we let the Chancery know we are in the area. Of course pastors do not need permission to make use of our services. I won't cite canon law to you."

"What canon do you have in mind?"

O'Halloran seemed not to hear. "Under the old code things were much different, of course."

"It's the old code I know best."

"There!" O'Halloran cried, as if he had proved a point. "In order to prepare a plan of action, we would have to sit down together and go over the books. What is your average Sunday collection, Father Dowling?"

Roger Dowling was certain O'Halloran would express shock if he gave him a number. The parish was self-supporting, barely, and neither he nor the parishioners hankered after upward mobility. When he was sent here, after more years than he liked to remember on the archdiocesan marriage tribunal, after succumbing to drink and dashing all hopes for clerical advancement, he knew that St. Hilary's was the clerical equivalent of Siberia. But from the very beginning, he had also known that he had at last come home. He loved this parish; he loved its people. It was past its prime, in transition, an area with large well-built family homes whose value had been drastically reduced by the freeways that now enclosed the parish in a triangle of concrete. Young couples were taking advantage of these bargains now, the number of children was growing, and perhaps in the future the parish school would be a school again and not a center where the elderly spent their days.

"I'm afraid we couldn't afford your services, Mr. O'Halloran."

"That's where you're wrong, Father. Unless you get something, we get nothing. We take ten percent after expenses."

"Tithing?"

O'Halloran beamed. "That's a good way of putting it."

"In any case, I am not your man. I am more than willing to let the Lord provide."

A look of mild reproach stole over the Irish face. "You wouldn't be falling into angelism, would you, Father?"

"Good angelism, I hope."

"We're creatures of flesh and blood, Father Dowling. Man does not live by the word alone."

"Is that St. Luke?"

"No, Father. That is St. Michael O'Halloran."

The fund raiser began a little homily on the incarnate nature of Christianity, but Roger Dowling cut him short. After forty-five minutes, even an Irishman's charm is not what it was.

"You seem half a priest yourself," Roger Dowling said as they went down the hall to the door.

"That's what my wife tells me," he said, and Roger Dowling saw a flicker of disappointment on Marie Murkin's face as she followed them from the kitchen door. "And do you know what I say to her?"

"I'm afraid to ask."

"Which half?" O'Halloran actually squeezed the priest's elbow. Roger Dowling tipped his head to one side and gave O'Halloran a look.

On the front porch, the little fund raiser asked Father Dowling to say a Mass for his mother, but then, looking toward the street, stopped.

"Great God almighty, look at that."

A large luxurious automobile stood at the curb, a magnificently American monster, all glitter and glass. But what caused O'Halloran's dismay was the sickening dip of the car. The rear wheel was flat.

"If I was alone I would swear," he said to the priest, and indeed his voice trembled as if he were nearer to tears than anger.

"And I wouldn't blame you. Come inside and we'll call a garage."

"A garage! Why, I'll change it myself."

He strode down the walk to the street and Father Dowling went along with him. At the car, O'Halloran pulled a ring of keys from his pocket and after several tries found the one that unlocked the door of the trunk. He twisted the key and the door popped open. O'Halloran leaned forward and then sprang back.

"Good God!"

"No jack?"

O'Halloran pointed and the priest went out into the street to look into the trunk.

The body lay on its side, nude except for jockey shorts. The sightless eyes stared straight ahead. The flesh was eerily white. There was little doubt that the man was dead.

TWO

THE MICHAEL O'HALLORAN who sat silently in a straight-back chair in the front parlor during the time it took Phil Keegan to come to the rectory was a far cry from the cocky little man who had tried to persuade Father Dowling that he could double the parish income in a matter of months.

"Who is the man, Michael?" Roger Dowling asked.

"I never saw him before."

"The car is your own?"

"It is."

"I wonder when . . ."

O'Halloran gave him a stricken look and shook his head. Was he wondering if the body had been put into the trunk while he was making his pitch to the pastor of St. Hilary's?

Roger Dowling said, "Do you suppose it all happened right here at St. Hilary's, while we were talking?" He could not help thinking that if this were the case, he could expect to be kept informed by Phil Keegan.

"That makes as much sense as anything else."

"When did you last look in your trunk?"

"Could you answer that question about yours?"

"You don't remember?"

"The last time I looked, there was no body in it."

"I'll have the housekeeper put on coffee."

"Thank you," O'Halloran said in a preoccupied way.

The pastor found Marie Murkin standing in the middle of her kitchen, wide-eyed, hands tightly clasped. Since hearing of the body in the trunk, she had been unable to do anything.

"Was it a man?" she spoke in a whisper, as if she might be overheard.

"A man in his underwear."

She clapped a hand over her mouth.

"I didn't recognize him, Marie. I am certain it is nobody from the parish." *Plane crash. No Catholics killed.* The old joke about a headline in the Catholic press.

When he went back to the front of the house, Phil had arrived and O'Halloran stood at the window, looking at the official cars that continued to arrive. The fund raiser handed Roger Dowling his keys.

"I'll wait here."

Who could blame the little man for not wanting to look again at the dead body in his trunk?

When the trunk was opened again, Phil stood in the street for some time, staring down at it, then stepped back while photographs were taken and the medical examiner's staff went to work.

"Abandoned?"

"No, no. The driver is in the rectory."

Phil started toward the house. Inside, he did not sit down when he was introduced to O'Halloran, nor did he offer to shake, although the little man leaned forward with an extended hand.

"That your car?"

O'Halloran looked to Father Dowling for an explanation of this rudeness. The pastor would not have wanted to explain to the fund raiser that Phil Keegan would have to know a lot more before he shook hands. He did not intend to greet someone who could turn out to be a murderer.

"The car is mine."

"Where you from?"

"Why do you ask?"

"The plates aren't the Chicago area."

"I'm from Peoria, Captain."

"When did you get to Fox River?"

"Yesterday."

"Where have you been since?"

He had driven from Peoria to Joliet. To visit the bishop. He turned to Roger Dowling. "A former client."

Phil asked what kind of work O'Halloran did and sat frowning through the explanation. Clearly he thought O'Halloran was some kind of charlatan.

"And you came here trying to involve Father Dowling in that kind of thing?"

O'Halloran decided that he would rather speak to the pastor. "I ran a thirty-day campaign in Joliet six months ago. I like to check up, to make sure the plan is being followed."

"What plan?" Phil asked.

"My involvement is just the beginning," O'Halloran said, still addressing Roger Dowling. "The follow-through is essential."

"Where did you stay last night, in Joliet?"

O'Halloran deigned to look at Phil. "I stayed in Oak Park last night."

"Where?"

"I have a unit at La Palomba."

Phil actually stepped back. "Why did you stay there?"

"In Oak Park?"

"At La Palomba!"

O'Halloran did not understand the question. "Why stay at a motel?"

"La Palomba is run by the mob, Mr. O'Halloran."

"The mob? What mob?"

"You've never heard of the mob?"

"Captain, as far as I'm concerned, it's just a motel."

"Who recommended it to you?"

"Nobody recommended it. I was looking for a motel; it caught my eye and I turned in. As far as I can see, it's exactly like every other motel."

"Yeah?"

The theory seemed to form effortlessly in Roger Dowling's mind. For whatever reason, let it be chance, O'Halloran stopped at a motel owned by the mob. It seemed plausible that his huge car had proved a tempting place to deposit the body of a murdered man.

"How do you know he was murdered?" O'Halloran asked.

"Experience. The medical examiner will bear me out."

Phil called a recess and went out to talk to the crew working on O'Halloran's rented car. They had finished the on-site examination and were removing the body. O'Halloran stood at the window, watching, shaking his head. When Phil turned to come back to the house, O'Halloran sat down again.

The victim had been struck a heavy blow just behind his right ear, but death had very likely been caused by strangulation. There were unmistakable signs that a cord had been twisted around the man's neck.

"Who is he, Phil?"

"It'll take a while to find out. Not much to go on."

"The poor devil," O'Halloran said.

"You're in trouble yourself," Phil said, but his heart was not in it. He had the look of a man who has been following the wrong scent.

"I never saw him before," O'Halloran said.

"You already told me that."

"It's important."

"You mean you wouldn't kill a perfect stranger?"

"Kill?" O'Halloran yelped. "I didn't kill anybody." He looked pleadingly at Father Dowling. "I can't believe this is happening to me."

The questioning went on for another hour. Cy Horvath came, and he and Phil took turns. Roger Dowling felt he was there as referee. It was difficult not to feel sorry for O'Halloran. For all the man's phoniness, he seemed genuinely distressed by what had happened, not just the inconvenience to himself, but what had happened to the still nameless victim. Meanwhile, the car outside was eased up a ramp into a police van and taken away for further study. Marie Murkin finally showed up with coffee. O'Halloran shook his head.

"Not unless it's decaf."

"There's some diet cola," Marie said, and the little fund raiser let his tongue loll from his mouth. Marie ultimately convinced him to try some celery juice and hurried away for it as soon as he agreed. The housekeeper had bought twenty dollars worth of items in a vegetarian store as an experiment, lured by the fountain-of-youth promises in the window. She had been trying to unload such things as celery juice and dandelion butter on the pastor ever since. She was certain that once she opened the celery juice, she would be able to persuade him to try it, but he told her he was not a herbivore. Marie was unable to throw out an unopened container of anything. O'Halloran's absentminded acceptance of celery juice might spare the recipients of the housekeeper's food donations next Thanksgiving.

"Did you get to know anyone at the motel, Mr. O'Halloran?"

He thought for half a minute. "I kidded with the waitress in the dining room. Before turning in I had a nightcap and talked with the bartender."

"You had a drink?"

"Yes."

"Just one?"

"No."

"How many?"

"They have a perpetual happy hour going in that place." Meaning that for every drink ordered, another was provided free. O'Halloran thought he had ordered three times. Six drinks? Well, Father Dowling thought, in his own drinking days that would have been nothing. But it was surprising that O'Halloran had been able to rise at an early hour and function all day. He certainly had not seemed the worse for wear earlier in the study. Cy wanted the names of the waitress and bartender, and O'Halloran got a little huffy at the suggestion he was not trusted.

"Who is going to provide me with a car? I cannot work without a car."

"Don't you have an expense account?"

"I don't see why Dasher Development should foot the bill because you have confiscated my car."

Keegan let a moment pass before answering. He did not like the suggestion that the Fox River police were inconveniencing O'Halloran. "You want Lieutenant Horvath to drop you somewhere?"

O'Halloran called a cab. It would be an ignominious departure when one thought of his arrival. Jollying Marie, talking a mile a minute to the pastor in his study, O'Halloran had been on top of the world. But ever since the discovery of the corpse, he had been like a deflated balloon. Cy left before O'Halloran's cab arrived, and Father Dowling accompanied the little fund raiser to the door. They shook hands, and O'Halloran's spirits revived.

"It just occurred to me, Father, that we could use this unfortunate incident as a springboard for a campaign." He snapped his fingers. "Just like that, St.

Hilary's is in the news. Thousands and thousands of dollars of free publicity..."

Roger Dowling put his hand on O'Halloran's arm. "You're going to make me think you brought that body on purpose."

O'Halloran adopted a theatrically horrified expression, then skipped down the walk to his waiting cab.

"Where's he staying tonight?" Phil asked when Roger Dowling came into the study. He had been invited to dinner and to watch the Bulls on television afterward.

"I didn't ask."

Phil watched the foam settle on his glass of beer. "I hope he's gone home to Peoria."

"And left his car here?"

"The La Palomba," Phil mused. "Imagine him spending the night there of all places. Maybe being from Peoria he hadn't known, but the look of the place should have told him something."

"What if he went back there?"

"Then he's dumber than he looks."

"Would he be in danger?"

"I told Cy to keep tabs on him."

"You mean protect him?"

Phil wiped his mouth with the back of his hand. "I hope it doesn't come to that."

The suggestion took a good deal of the enjoyment out of the basketball game for Roger Dowling. The image of O'Halloran hopping into a cab and being driven away into danger troubled him. Had Phil hoped he would go back to La Palomba? Roger Dowling tried to take comfort from the thought of Cy Horvath watching over the little Irishman.

Suddenly there was O'Halloran on the television screen. It was halftime, there was a break for local news, and O'Halloran was being interviewed by a young woman whose manner suggested that she was speaking with a man of importance, if not stature. She paused to tell the camera that she was interviewing Michael O'Halloran, in the trunk of whose car a dead body had been found earlier in the day. She turned to the celebrity.

"Could you describe your emotions when you opened your trunk?"

The cocky confidence O'Halloran had shown in the study was back. O'Halloran's eye moved unerringly from the interviewer to the camera lens as he described the horror he had felt when he saw what was in his trunk.

"Was it a man or woman?"

"I'll tell you something, my dear, and let sexists make of it what they will. I didn't notice. Not at first. If I had slammed the door down immediately, I could not have said whether I had seen the body of a man or a woman. As it happens, it was a man's body."

"Fully clothed?"

"My dear, he wore nothing but skivvies. Shorts. Underwear. Plum-colored shorts of the briefest kind."

"Did this happen here at the motel?"

The shot widened, and it became clear that O'Halloran was being interviewed in the parking lot of a motel. A gaudy neon sign came into view. La Palomba. Phil Keegan sputtered with anger.

"That idiot will get himself killed."

O'Halloran was now confiding to the television audience that he had been visiting his good friend Father Dowling, the pastor of St. Hilary's church out in Fox River, to speak of the parish finances. After a pleasant visit, despite the fact that it was a business call, he had come out of the rectory to find he had a flat tire. He opened the trunk and got the surprise of his life.

"Your car had a flat?"

"Quite a coincidence, wasn't it? Obviously somebody wanted me to find the body there."

"Somebody? Who do you think it was?"

The televised O'Halloran looked at the young lady as if he had decided to spare her tender ears.

"Whoever put the body in the trunk," he said.

"They'll kill him," Keegan growled. "Let me use your phone."

He called downtown and was put through by radio to Cy Horvath. He said something short and profane, but then fell silent, listening.

"Okay. But get him out of there, Cy."

"He can bring O'Halloran here," Father Dowling said.

"Are you serious?"

"Marie has a crush on him."

"Bring him here if you can, Cy, but get him out of there," Keegan said into the phone, then hung up. "What do you mean about Marie?"

"I think O'Halloran stole her heart away."

"The man's a dwarf!"

"Marie's no Amazon."

Phil puffed moodily on his cigar. There was something unstated between Phil and Marie, but Father Dowling could not bring himself to tease either of them about it. After a minute, Phil said. "O'Halloran is married."

"You better warn Marie."

THREE

THE WOMAN CAME OUT of the side door of the church as Father Dowling emerged from the rectory on his way to say the noon Mass. She advanced toward him a few steps and then, seeing he was coming toward her, decided to wait where she was. Indeed, as he approached, she stepped back under the Gothic arch.

Even from a distance, Roger Dowling had noted the resemblance. He might have thought it was O'Halloran himself in a bizarre disguise if the woman had not been taller, and attractive, even beautiful. The features that were scrunched into comic compression on O'Halloran's face were proportioned and graceful on hers.

"Father Dowling?"

"Is it Miss O'Halloran?"

Her smile was a little resigned. "Is it so obvious? My name *was* O'Halloran. Do you have a minute?"

"Not just now, I'm afraid. I say Mass at noon." Even as he spoke the quarter hour sounded above them, the sonorous bell a recording that could be heard for miles when the traffic on the interstate was subdued. "Could you join me for lunch afterward?"

"Let me take you to lunch."

"Mrs. Murkin wouldn't like that. Everything will be ready to serve when I get back. You'll have to be my guest."

"I'll come to Mass." She said it as if he might contradict her.

"Good."

He could have given her a minute then, but he did not like to break his habit of recollecting himself thoroughly before saying Mass. It was his chief function as a priest, saying Mass, and he did not want it to become mere routine. But that day he was constantly distracted by the prospect of speaking with O'Halloran's daughter. He had not even asked what she had come to him for, but it had to be about her father.

"Are there always so many at daily Mass?" she asked when he came out of the sacristy afterward. She was waiting for him where he had first seen her.

"More or less."

"My grandmother went to Mass every day."

The suggestion was that her parents had not and, *a fortiori,* neither did she. She might have been commenting on the attrition that afflicts the passing on of the faith. Religious faith cannot be inherited, and how it is transmitted is one of the deeper mysteries. Family and upbringing were thought to explain it, and perhaps sometimes they did. But not always.

"You're married?" he asked as they crossed to the rectory. Roger Dowling saw Marie Murkin in the kitchen window. So she would have forewarning that there was a guest for lunch.

"My name is Maureen Dilthey. We have two children."

"Do you live in Peoria?"

"Oh no. In Barrington."

"That close?"

"You mean to Fox River? It's not close to Peoria, thank God."

He let it go. Inside the house, Marie gave a reasonable imitation of a welcome and they went on to the dining room, where bowls of split pea soup were soon set before them. Maureen looked around the room.

"I don't think I've been in a rectory since before I got married."

He said grace and she bowed her head. Afterwards, she looked at him.

"It's been a long time since I did that too.'

"Is your husband Catholic?"

He regretted the question as soon as he asked it. She became wary. "Did you and Dad talk about me?"

"No."

"I know he was here. Did you know he was on television last night? He gave you a plug."

"I saw the interview."

"Was all that true? Was there a dead body in the trunk of his car?"

"I saw it myself." Did she think her father would make up a story like that for a television reporter? When Marie came to take away their bowls, he told her that Maureen was the daughter of Mr. O'Halloran. The housekeeper nodded, avoiding the young woman's eyes. Was she afraid Maureen would guess she had been all but swept off her feet by her fast-talking father?

"I see the resemblance."

"Did he sign you up?" Maureen asked Roger Dowling. Clearly she did not think much of her father's trade.

"No."

"Meaning not yet? He is really very good at what he does. It's certainly the right job for him."

"How so?"

"It's churchy. He is a pretty ferocious Catholic."

"I suppose the church has been good to him."

He sensed that it would take time for her to say why she had come. Seeing her father on television, hearing the mention of St. Hilary's, explained only how she had known where to come.

"You said you saw the body, Father?"

"Yes."

She had taken cigarettes from her purse. "Do you mind if I smoke?"

"I insist on it. Then I can light my pipe."

When the dining room was satisfyingly full of smoke, she said, "Was it the body of a man?"

"Yes."

She took a deep drag on her cigarette. "Who was he?"

"Your father didn't know him."

"Hasn't he been identified?"

"Not yet I don't think." He sent a smoke ring toward the ceiling. "The theory is that it was a gangland killing. Your father was staying in a very dangerous place."

"He made that clear enough on television."

"He shouldn't have done that."

"Why?"

"It was unwise to draw the attention of certain people to himself. And to draw attention to them."

She laughed. "But that is my father's stock in trade, drawing attention."

He had thought her earlier concern was worry for her father, but her reaction did not support that. Had she thought her father might be in some way responsible for the dead man? Her dismissal of the possibility of gangland reprisals suggested she had no fear for her father's safety.

"Why did you come see me, Maureen?"

"You've put off asking that question a long time, haven't you?"

"Should I put it off longer?"

"I'm not a very good Catholic. Not at all like my father. I don't mean to blame him for it." Meaning he was the explanation, at least in part. "I feel bad about my kids."

"Is your husband Catholic?"

"He was. He's not much of anything anymore."

"That's a pretty sweeping statement."

"Life isn't what we think it's going to be, is it, Father?"

"I guess not. Someone called life a book in which we set out to write one story and end by writing another."

She nodded. "I came here because it was so close. It's in my blood. O'Hallorans worry about one another. I had to find out about Dad." She put out her cigarette and picked up her purse. "You've been very kind, Father."

"Now that you know how to find the place, I hope you'll come back."

"Only if I can take you to lunch."

"Fair enough."

Her station wagon was in the school parking lot, and Father Dowling watched her go off down the sidewalk to it. Her visit puzzled him. The point of it had never emerged, unless of course her lapsed status was the reason and her father's appearance on the late-night news merely an excuse to come talk with a priest.

FOUR

THE BODY IN THE TRUNK belonged to Morton Upton, address on the near north side, five blocks inland from the lake. He lived alone and had been at the current address for three years.

"No family?"

"Apparently not. He worked for a computing firm in Skokie." Phil glanced at Cy Horvath, who took a notebook from his pocket and opened it.

"Not much on his personnel form. Born in El Paso, graduated from high school in St. Louis, where he attended a technical college."

"How old was he?"

"Thirty-one."

"No next of kin?"

"He had listed a woman in St. Louis, an aunt, but she died two years ago. We learned that when we tried to reach her."

"All alone in the world," Roger Dowling said sadly.

Cy looked at the ceiling. "Not quite."

"How so?"

Phil cleared his throat. "The man had the reputation of a swinger, Roger. When he wasn't working, he was seducing women. He hung around singles bars. Thirty-one years old and he hadn't grown up."

"Do you think that has something to do with his death?"

Phil shrugged. "Maybe. The way he lived, he had no friends, no one close. Every night everything was brand new. His face was familiar to bartenders, but none of them knew him, not really."

"He was last seen in a place called The Toadstool." Cy was consulting his notebook. "Two nights ago, maybe three, maybe even four. No one remembers who he was with, if anybody."

"Had he been to work since then?"

"He worked the day before his body was found."

THAT HAD BEEN on Wednesday. Phil and Cy had come by the rectory on the off chance that O'Halloran might be there. Phil was convinced the little Irishman would try to persuade Roger Dowling to sign up for a fund-raising effort. O'Halloran had dropped from sight after his televised interview, not even spending the night at La Palomba, eluding the watchful eye of Cy Horvath. His car had been released to him on Tuesday, but he was long gone by the time Phil Keegan was told. No reason he should have been notified—he hadn't left word to that effect, something he blamed himself for later.

"Could something have happened to him?"

"Giving the interview was dumb, but ever since he's been acting smart. Keeping out of sight is a good idea."

They wanted to talk to O'Halloran about Upton, to see if by any chance he had known the man. It seemed to be just one of the remote possibilities that had to be checked out in the interests of thoroughness when there were no lively leads. Cy Horvath wanted to know what exactly O'Halloran did for a living. Roger Dowling tried to explain without making what O'Halloran did sound like something that might interest the bunko squad.

"Where is Dasher located?"

Roger Dowling produced the brochure O'Halloran had left with him and handed it to Phil.

"Cy, how about going out there and seeing if they can tell us where O'Halloran is."

"I hope nobody has beat me to it."

Phil frowned. "I suppose I could call Peoria."

"And frighten his wife?" Maureen's visit somehow suggested the family was keeping tabs on the little fund raiser. "What will happen to the body, Phil?"

"My God, I hope it hasn't come to that."

"I mean Morton Upton's. If you're that concerned, maybe you should call his wife."

Phil shook his head. "I'd rather check with the Peoria police first."

ROGER DOWLING made arrangements for Upton's burial and accompanied the body to the grave. It was a melancholy journey, just himself and two men from the undertaker's. The three of them rode side by side in the front seat of the hearse.

"Was he a parishioner of yours, Father?" The pink- and chubby-cheeked undertaker was just making conversation.

"No. Are many people buried like this?"

"Without mourners? It happens. County business, usually, but generally those are cremations." He glanced at Roger Dowling. "Non-Catholics."

A bright day in early November, the leaves turning, doomed and glorious. They might have been trying to give death a good name. The two undertakers carried the coffin across the grass to the newly dug grave. There were no markers on these plots. Upton too would be going into an unmarked grave.

He read some hopeful passages of Scripture over the coffin, wondering if Upton had believed in God. Well, he had been God's creature in any case, and the priest prayed the reunion was a happy one.

When he was done, he turned and saw that a car had pulled up ahead of the undertaker's hearse and not really stopped, but was inching along the road. It caught shafts of sunlight threading through the trees. Roger Dowling was sure it was the station wagon in which Maureen Dilthey had come to St. Hilary's.

A large, lean rust-colored dog rose inquisitively at the appearance of Roger Dowling's car and began to describe a wide arc across the lawn, as if meaning to surprise the car, but from time to time emitting a questioning bark. The barking became continuous as Roger Dowling continued up the long driveway toward the small house set on a hill. After he stopped the engine, he waited behind the wheel to see if someone would be drawn outside by the dog. There was no sign of the car he had seen at the cemetery.

Despite the fact that the sun lay on the large picture window, the priest saw someone move inside. He got out of the car so he could be recognized. In such an isolated house, Maureen Dilthey would have reason to be wary, as the presence of the dog testified.

The front door of the house opened, but it was a man who came out into the sunlight. He was large, and looked larger standing on the porch of the small house. Roger Dowling raised a hand in greeting, and the man responded by summoning the dog. The animal seemed relieved that the stranger need no longer be feared, and he went at a gallop toward the man.

"Mr. Dilthey?" Father Dowling called.

His face was full but long, too, and his reddish hair was slicked back in an old-fashioned way. The priest was going to take silence for assent when the man spoke. "Wilhelm."

"My name is Father Dowling."

"My father-in-law's friend?" The tone was sardonic. Roger Dowling tried to think of a way to explain this visit. It did not seem wise to mention that Maureen had come to see him.

"Michael O'Halloran? Yes, he came to see me."

"We saw it on the news."

"Have you seen Mr. O'Halloran?"

Dilthey's eyes were like marbles partially emerging from their pouches. "If you expected to find him here, you're wasting your time."

"Have you seen him lately?"

"Not since that television interview."

"He hinted he was in danger."

Dilthey was amused by the suggestion. "Mike likes to be dramatic."

"I've just come from burying the man who was found in his trunk." Roger Dowling had been moving toward Dilthey during this exchange and now stood at the foot of the porch steps.

"Who was he?"

"They found out his name but it doesn't help to explain what happened. It was sadder than most funerals, just myself and the men from the undertaker."

But Dilthey was distracted. He was looking beyond Father Dowling. The priest turned, and the car he had seen at the cemetery was coming up the driveway. Maureen Dilthey was at the wheel. She came to a stop behind the priest's car, and then backed into a turnaround. The dog ran to meet her and frisked and frolicked about like a puppy as she strode toward the house, a look of concern on her face.

"Has something happened to my father?"

He should have expected his presence to suggest bad news, but it was an occupational hazard he had never gotten used to. He assured her that, so far as he knew, Michael O'Halloran was all right.

"I haven't seen him, however. The police have been wanting to talk with him since the body was identified, but I don't believe they have succeeded in finding him yet."

"With Dad, no news is good news, Father."

"You don't know where he might be?"

She shook her head. Now she seemed no more concerned about Michael O'Halloran than her husband had been.

"I visited Father Dowling the other day," she said to her husband, and suggested they go inside.

Dilthey had just put on fresh coffee, and the house was filled with its aroma. Beyond the dining room was another room through whose open door the screen of a computer glowed greenly.

"Do you work at home?"

"Today I do. The computer is down." He was an accountant for a medical clinic in Barrington. "Fortunately, I have everything backed up that I need."

"I wish I understood computers," Roger Dowling said.

Dilthey opened his hands. "I don't understand them. I only know how to use them."

"Could I see it?"

The question seemed to justify his visit, but he had no idea that it would call forth such a didactic strain in the burly redhead. Not that Dilthey was a good teacher. Explanations tumbled out one after the other, forming an unintelligible hodgepodge. The narrative was accompanied by pecking away at the keyboard. Columns of figures formed and reformed on the screen.

"How marvelous," Roger Dowling said.

"When it works. As I said, the office computer is down."

"What do you do then?"

"Call the repairman," Maureen said from the doorway, and her husband turned to look at her.

She said, "I'll walk you to your car, Father. Bill can be such a bore."

"We offered him a cup of coffee."

Roger Dowling assumed a noncommittal smile. Although they had said little to one another, he had the sense he was witnessing a quarrel between the Diltheys. He suspected that Michael O'Halloran must be a bone of contention in this house.

"Would you like coffee, Father?" she asked.

He looked at his watch. "I've just come from a funeral," he said. "It was a wild thought, I suppose, that I might find your father here."

"Not so wild as all that." She moved toward the kitchen, and he followed her. "Do you have a cup in there, Bill?"

"It's next to the pot."

She filled her husband's mug first and took it in to him. From the kitchen window, Roger Dowling looked out on the lawn that sloped toward the road. The dog lay under a walnut tree, tongue lolling, keeping a lazy eye on the traffic. Maureen Dilthey came back.

"Cream or sugar?"

"Black. Just half a cup."

"I have some instant decaffeinated."

"No!"

She did not have any herself and seemed to be waiting for him to drink his. He sipped it several times and put it down. Almost immediately, she led him through the house to the front door.

Outside, halfway to his car, she said, "You came because you saw me at the cemetery, didn't you?"

"Well, I did notice your car."

"I called you, and Mrs. Murkin told me about the funeral. By the time I got there it was over, so I just kept going."

"But you wanted to come?"

"It seemed so sad. To be found dead like that and then be buried without anyone to care." Tears welled in her eyes. "Life doesn't make a lot of sense, does it?"

"Not always."

She turned toward the house and then seemed to survey the land on which it stood. "Sometimes I imagine what it was like on this very spot four or five hundred years ago. A thousand years ago. Isn't it eerie to think that places go on and on while people come and go?"

A line of Eliot's formed in his head. *Birth, copulation, death.* But did that really sum up human life?

"People are created to outlast all places, Maureen."

"You really believe that?"

"Especially on days when I conduct funerals."

"My father didn't attend."

"Did you expect to see him there?"

She didn't answer, and they continued on to his car. She looked at her watch.

"It's almost time for me to get the kids."

"They're in school?"

"Only one. The other's in preschool."

She stood with folded arms, watching him drive away, an enigmatic figure framed in his rearview mirror. She could have come to the funeral of Morton Upton to see her father as well as out of compas-

sion for the unknown victim. Michael O'Halloran
was as likely to be there as she was. But at least half
her reason had to be what she had said; to be there
when a man without relations and friends was lowered into the earth.

FIVE

WHEN PHIL CAME BY LATER, he told Roger Dowling that Michael O'Halloran was home in Peoria. Meanwhile, the investigation into Morton Upton continued, with one significant result.

"He was known at La Palomba, Roger."

"Really?"

"Cy showed his picture, discreetly of course, to some of the help, the cleaning women, and sure enough, he had stayed there. With various women."

"A place of assignation?"

"He took women there," Keegan said gruffly.

"So that explains it."

"Explains what?" Phil had unwrapped a cigar and was licking it into shape before lighting it.

"His being there."

"I thought you meant his being dead."

Roger put on his topcoat, managing to conceal that this was not as easy an operation as it once had been. He seemed to be experiencing the beginnings of arthritis and was determined to keep it a secret. He and Phil were on their way to the Rosemont Horizon, where DePaul was playing its home opener, and

Roger hoped his knees would not stiffen up in the snug seats of the arena.

Phil drove an unmarked car equipped with a radio, and on the way the constant chatter of police traffic provided a background for their conversation. The incessant litany of human misbehavior made the mindless involvement in a basketball game even more attractive. Beneath the civilized crust of society was the teeming world of crime. Of course, it was crime among the lower classes that made the police radio band. Unless, that is, a member of the middle class like Morton Upton, a wizard of the computer, whose misbehavior would normally go unchronicled, ended up dead in a trunk.

"So Morton Upton was killed at La Palomba and his body dumped into the trunk of O'Halloran's car?"

"Is that your theory, Roger?"

"I'm asking if it's yours."

Phil's cigar was clenched between teeth exposed in the sardonic smile he usually wore while driving. He nodded. "It could have happened that way."

"Just could have?"

"He wasn't registered at the motel that night."

"And of course the records at La Palomba are above reproach."

"The reason we discovered he stayed there was the cleaning ladies, but before he had registered. The manager was glad to show Cy his records."

"And equally glad to show he had not been registered on the night he died? What did you learn from the cleaning crew about that?"

Cy had thought they were telling him Upton had been staying in the motel on the fatal night but subsequent questioning encountered lapses of memory and a general unwillingness to cooperate with the police. On the first occasion they had thought Cy was an irate husband in pursuit of his wife's lover.

"Then he could have been at La Palomba that night?"

"Sure. I'm assuming he was. Whether he was there alive is something else."

"But surely the body was put in O'Halloran's trunk while his car was parked at La Palomba the night he stayed there."

Keegan nodded, but it was a noncommittal nod. Roger Dowling puffed on his pipe. The first explanation seemed the last. O'Halloran's trunk had been used to get rid of a body. The next morning, the little man drove away, and somewhere else, Peoria perhaps, days later when the odor became intense, the body would be found.

It seemed a good enough explanation. But Roger Dowling realized that he was no more comfortable with it than Phil. No matter. They were entering the parking lot of the Rosemont Horizon, and the prospect of a great game lay before them.

THE BLUE DEMONS and Joey triumphed, and it was going on midnight when Phil drew up before the St. Hilary rectory in Fox River. Roger Dowling was surprised when Phil shut off the engine.

"That's Cy's car, Roger." He pointed to the car parked in the deep shadow of the parish school.

And indeed when they got out of the car, there was the sound of another door slamming, and the huge figure of Cy Horvath came toward them into the light of the street lamp.

"What is it, Cy?"

"I got hold of Upton's work record."

"Anything show up?"

If Cy's face was a map of Hungary, it was featureless as always. "I figure I'll start checking out the places he worked. He did a lot of on the spot jobs for various companies."

Phil looked at Roger Dowling and the priest nodded. Obviously this was excuse enough to go inside. At the sound of the three men, Marie Murkin descended into the kitchen from her apartment in the back of the house and insisted on making cocoa. Only Cy greeted this suggestion gladly.

"I'll have a beer, Marie," Phil said.

"It's much too late for a beer. You probably filled yourself with junk food at the game."

"I did have some cocoa."

It was cocoa or nothing, so that is what they had, marshmallows bobbing on the chocolate surface. Roger had never before seen Cy so expressive. Something very like a smile disturbed the smooth surface of his face when there was a telltale line of chocolate on his lips. But he handed the sheets of computer print-out to Phil, who laid them on the desk in the study so that he and the pastor could study them.

"What am I looking for, Cy?" Phil asked after several minutes.

"That's what I want to know. Obviously it is a long shot. You want me to check them all out?"

"I don't have any better ideas."

"Neither do I."

Roger Dowling saw the entry on the last page, and turning back he saw that the Barrington firm appeared several times. Medicure Inc. Where Dilthey was an accountant. Morton Upton had been sent there to develop a billing system for the clinic. Would Cy Horvath learn that Dilthey was O'Halloran's son-in-law? Not before Roger Dowling had a chance to find out if this was pure coincidence or something else.

"More cocoa, Phil?" he asked.

"Give me a break."

"Is there more?" Cy asked, and Marie appeared in the doorway with a tea kettle in one hand and a packet in the other.

"One is enough for you, Phillip, but Lieutenant Horvath deserves another."

WHEN HIS GUESTS were gone, Roger Dowling sat on in his study, only the desk lamp on, smoking a final pipe before going upstairs. Compsultants of Chicago and Medicure of Barrington. The link between the two companies was a link between Upton and Dilthey. Dilthey was a link to Michael O'Halloran who worked for Dasher Development, which is why he showed up at the St. Hilary rectory with the body of Morton Upton in his trunk. O'Halloran had spent the night at La Palomba Motel in Oak Park, where the swinger Upton had often registered with various women. La Palomba had connections with the mob. A body in a trunk clad only in what O'Halloran had called plum-colored shorts suggested a gangland slaying.

The priest leaned back in his chair and watched smoke rise out of the reach of the desklamp's glow. There were so many connections, but finally the whole thing seemed to disappear into murkiness. He put his pipe in an ashtray and turned out the desklamp as if total darkness would clarify his thoughts.

Would Maureen O'Halloran Dilthey care to take him to lunch tomorrow?

HE MET HER AFTER his noon Mass at an Italian restaurant called Montini's in a mall in Barrington. It was crowded, with suburban wives and businessmen in roughly equal proportion. No wonder if the linguini he ordered was typical. It was delicious. Maureen had red wine with her cannelloni, but Roger Dowling ordered mineral water.

"It's one of the few times I miss drinking. When I have Italian food."

"Wine isn't drinking."

"For me it is."

"Oh."

He had not meant it to, but that revelation of his own flaw removed a barrier between them. He felt that long before she began to speak freely.

"I told you things were not going well for us. For Bill and me. I don't mean just religion."

"There's more to life than religion."

"When you asked about Bill, I wondered if Dad had talked about me with you."

"I remember your asking."

"It's a wonder we haven't broken up. If it weren't for the kids . . ."

"What's the problem?"

"Me." Her eyes opened wide with anguish. Then she leaned toward him and spoke rapidly in a low voice. "I tell myself to grow up, to count my blessings and be content. Bill has a good job, the kids are wonderful, so what is it I want? I wish I knew. All I know is that I expected more from life than a house in Barrington and a couple of kids and a solid husband and a succession of days exactly like one another."

The Romantic agony. He did not say it. Nor did he feel condescending toward her. The human heart was made for far more than this world can give.

"I've been unfaithful."

"I see."

"Do you?"

"Morton Upton?"

Her eyes searched his for a full minute. What was she looking for? Blame, forgiveness, understanding, doubt? Perhaps all of them. Finally she nodded slowly as she formed the word silently but could not speak it. Yes.

One wall of the restaurant faced the concourse of the mall, and through a window Roger Dowling could see a constant stream of people pass. Every life is a drama of infinite importance. What Maureen told him was trite, but of course to her it could not be an anonymous contribution to a statistic. She had been unfaithful to her husband, betrayed her marriage and her children, and with someone she was far from loving.

"He was so shallow. The way he talked! He would have been perfect on a television game show, with his mannerisms and turns of speech. What you see is what you get. That was one of his deathless remarks, endlessly repeated. How true it was. There was no depth, no..." She stopped. "I am not trying to excuse myself. Far from it. I cannot say I was swept off my feet, nothing like that. I would rather spend a week with Bill than an hour with that silly man. He was a figment of my imagination."

She meant she had cast him for a role he did not fit. Of course the first time he came to the house to work on her husband's computer, she did not know anything about him. That he knew his job was clear enough. He was attractive in an immature sort of way, but she was a wife and mother, and besides, Wilhelm was home, and she was never alone with Upton. For all she knew, he hadn't even noticed her. But he had.

"He had a sixth sense, Father. Somehow he knew how weak I am, how plagued by dreams. He just drove in one day after I had come back from taking the kids to school. I opened the door, and he came in and..."

She worked her lips, and tears stood in her eyes. It is not easy to admit to oneself that one has done wrong, but to tell another can take real courage.

"Now you know why I went to his funeral. I don't know if he believed in sin or thought there is an afterlife. We never *talked,* not about anything important."

"How often did you see him?"

"Once a week, over a period of two months. This is like making my confession, isn't it?"

"Yes, it is."

"I want it to be."

"When did you see him last?"

"It's been almost a month." She made a face. "Twenty-seven days. I made up my mind never to see him again, I stayed away from the house, I didn't answer the phone. I have never eaten so many unwanted lunches or done so much shopping. Well, it worked. And then he is found dead in my father's car!"

He waited for her to go on. Surely she saw that her affair with Morton Upton would seem to provide the clue to events that otherwise dissolved into coincidence.

"Would you say a Mass for him, Father?"

"Of course."

A pained little smile formed on her face. "I sound like my father."

"Did he know about Upton?"

"No!"

"When you asked if he had spoken of you to me, what did you think he might say?"

"That I wasn't practicing my religion. They celebrated their thirty-fifth anniversary last month. There was a big Mass, and my parents renewed their vows with a dozen priests and a bishop in the sanctuary. He noticed that I didn't receive Communion. Everyone else did, even Bill, even my brother George whose first marriage was never annulled. I wonder if Dad spoke to George about that?"

"He spoke to you?"

"He asked me why I hadn't received Communion. I told him I was not worthy. I actually quoted. 'O Lord, I am not worthy.'"

O'Halloran had been furious at her flip tone and assured her that no one was worthy. Had he wanted her to tell him she had committed a serious sin and not confessed it? Roger Dowling could all too easily imagine the little fund raiser grilling his daughter about the condition of her soul. She had called him a ferocious Catholic.

"But you didn't tell him about Morton Upton?"

"Father, I would rather tear out my tongue than admit a thing like that to Michael O'Halloran. You met him. You must have seen what he is like. If there has ever been anyone who played strictly according to the rules, it is my father.''

Unfortunately, that could mean either that one acted as he should or that one was a Pharisee.

When they left the restaurant, there were only two people still there, a couple at a table in a far corner of the room. Maureen looked at them ruefully. Did she wonder if it was an illicit couple, like Morton Upton and herself? However unfortunate her affair had been, it had made a profound impression on her, and Father Dowling could imagine her becoming an extraordinary person because of it. Many saints had started on their way by falling into sin.

''Does that really count as confession, Father?''

He had her sit beside him in his car. Slipping a stole around his shoulders, he gave her absolution. The occasion seemed to call for a slight bending of the rules. There were tears in her eyes when she said goodbye.

''Don't forget to say that Mass for him.''

He assured her he would remember.

That she had told him what she had in confidence would have sufficed for him to keep quiet about it. Besides, he really did not know what Maureen's affair with Upton explained. Wilhelm Dilthey had not known of his wife's dalliance, at least she was certain he had not. Even if he could be shown to be a wronged husband, there was no way to connect him with the body in his father-in-law's car. It was still possible that Morton Upton had been done in by mobsters and dumped into Michael O'Halloran's trunk. Of course it was possible. "And I am Marie of Roumania," as Dorothy Parker wrote.

He was scheduled to take part in Forty Hours Devotion at Father George Clement's parish in Chicago that night, and afterward he stayed later than he normally would have in the upstairs parlor of the Holy Angels parish house, the room done all in black and white. The clerical gossip was diverting, and it was quite late when he arrived home in Fox River. A note on his desk indicated that Phil Keegan had called.

He managed to avoid Phil for two complete days, and when they did get together for a game of cribbage late on Friday night, there was no news on the Morton Upton murder. In fact, if Roger Dowling had not brought up the subject, it would not have arisen.

"We're just slogging through the routine, Father. This may be one we just aren't meant to solve."

"Did you see tonight's paper?"

An editorial complained that the mob was dropping its dirty linen in Fox River and doing it with impunity. Chief Robertson had announced that they had no leads and seemed to suggest none would be found. The editorialist hinted darkly that local police were intimidated by the reputation of those likely to be involved.

"What a bunch of bunk, Roger. The manager of La Palomba called and offered me any cooperation. They want this thing cleared up."

"Meaning they are not involved."

"That's the idea."

"So what is Cy doing?"

"He is going to talk with Upton's clients one by one."

Which meant that he would certainly talk to Wilhelm Dilthey. But it seemed doubtful now that Cy would discover the link between Dilthey's wife and the murdered man. No wonder Phil found it difficult to believe that they were likely to find the murderer of Morton Upton.

The following day, the routine investigation Cy had been pursuing suddenly seemed pointless. In Peoria, a bomb went off in Michael O'Halloran's car.

SIX

MICHAEL O'HALLORAN had not been seriously injured. In fact, he had been the beneficiary of what appeared to be a miracle. The bomb had gone off before he got into the car. He had just backed his wife's Omega into the drive and shut the garage door when the explosion occurred. The door was blown out by the force of the blast, and O'Halloran was found lying beneath it by a neighbor who had been awakened by the sound of the car backing out of the garage and wondered what was going on at that hour.

"This was like five in the morning, Roger," Phil said.

"A bomb in his car?"

"I know what you're thinking. It's what Robertson thinks too. It's got to be the mob."

"What do you think?"

"Why did he get out to shut the door? It could have been done with the remote control in his wife's car."

Roger Dowling just stared at Phil. The detail was one Cy Horvath would have noticed, but what significance did it really have? The priest realized that he himself was elated to have attention diverted away from the Diltheys. How awful it would have been to have that affair revealed, now that it was definitively over and Maureen herself had broken it off and repented of it.

"More important, Roger. What's the motive for the mob?"

Revenge? Roger Dowling did not know. He said nothing. It was effort enough to stop himself from letting out a cheer.

"Most important is something else."

"What's that?"

"If it was the mob, O'Halloran wouldn't still be alive."

However Phil Keegan and Cy Horvath might resist the implications of the bombing in Peoria, Roger Dowling was sure that Chief Robertson's view would prevail. The death of Morton Upton as well as the bombing of Michael O'Halloran's car would be laid at the door of the mob. And just lie there. It did not seem too high a price to pay for Maureen Dilthey's peace of mind.

Roger Dowling drove down to Peoria to visit O'Halloran in the hospital. A policeman sat in a chair outside the door of O'Halloran's room. The patient wore a turban bandage around his head but seemed otherwise in good repair.

"They are keeping me for observation, Father. With these nurses, I told them I'd be glad to." He waggled his brows and winked at an overweight Florence Nightingale, from whose starched cap coal black ringlets showed, mementos of her lost youth.

"You are lucky to be alive."

"Amen to that, Father. I was wearing the brown scapular at the time. Maybe that's why I'm still here."

"They will try again."

O'Halloran thought about it. He seemed unconcerned. "No, Father, I don't think so."

"Why not?"

"Call it a hunch."

Phil Keegan would call it something else, the priest reflected, and he tended to agree with Phil. The bombing had been delayed retaliation for that stupid televised interview in the parking lot of La Palomba. Such people could be patient. What was the saying? Don't get mad, get even. Was Maureen's good name to be bought at the price of her father's life?

"I met your daughter."

"Which one?"

"Maureen. Mrs. Dilthey."

O'Halloran's puckish smile seemed to freeze on his freckled face. "Did you now?"

"She came to see me. Thanks to your mention on television, she knew how to find me."

"And what did she want, Father?"

"This was the day after your call on me. She was concerned about you."

"So you had a good talk, I suppose."

"I've met Wilhelm too."

O'Halloran nodded and his expression indicated pleasure at hearing this, but his eyes were ice cold.

"Even the best of marriages have their troubles, Father."

"I'm sure that's true."

"The persons involved lack perspective. Things can look much worse than they are."

Roger Dowling felt they were conversing in code. He assumed O'Halloran was alluding to his daughter's lukewarm Catholicism. In any case, he wanted to change whatever the subject was.

"You must come again to St. Hilary's and tell me what Dasher Development could do for the parish."

"Father, this is a bit heretical, but let me say that I wouldn't change anything about St. Hilary's. Critics would say you're in a time warp, a little pocket of preconciliar Catholicism."

"I hope no one accepts Vatican II more wholeheartedly than I do."

"The critics, Father, not I. No, I don't think you need the services of Dasher Development."

"I agree there wouldn't be much in it for you."

O'Halloran adopted a wounded expression. "You see what honesty brings on a man! Just for that I *will* come again and try to talk you into something you don't need. How is Captain Keegan?"

"Still investigating the murder of Morton Upton."

"This bombing should tell him where to look."

"The police are champions of routine. They are looking into Upton's past, his work records, interviewing all his clients."

"What a waste of time!" He seemed angry.

"You may be right. Mrs. Murkin sends her regards."

"Mrs. Murkin?"

"My housekeeper."

"Oh, yes."

Marie would not be flattered to learn how fleeting an impression she had made on the little Irishman. But she did want to hear all about the patient.

"Won't they try to kill him again, Father?"

"He doesn't think so."

"Why not?"

"He says it's a hunch."

She shook her head. "The Irish always think they're so lucky. I hope he's right. I also hope the police down there keep an eye on him."

Two days later, Phil Keegan stopped by at midafternoon.

"I can't stay, Roger. I wonder if you could come with me."

"What is it?"

"O'Halloran."

"Good Lord! What's happened to him?"

"At the moment he is being arraigned. He showed up several hours ago to confess to the murder of Morton Upton."

"What!"

"He insists on seeing you. Of course he's crazy, but he sure makes a convincing case against himself."

"That man couldn't kill a flea," Marie Murkin announced from the kitchen doorway. "It's plain as can be why he's come to you with that story, Phillip Keegan."

"Is it?"

"It is. He is afraid of another bombing and thinks he will be safer in jail."

Phil looked at Roger Dowling. "That's as good an explanation as I can think of."

Roger Dowling was not prepared for the crestfallen Irishman Michael O'Halloran had become. They were left alone at O'Halloran's insistence.

"I can tell you what I can't tell them, Father. You understand I am speaking under the seal. If you have a stole with you, I'll make it a proper confession."

"That would certainly guarantee you were telling the truth."

"I refer to why I killed the man, Father. My guess is you already know. That Maureen told you." He rubbed his face with both hands and looked abjectly at the priest. "Father, that man seduced Maureen. He came to the house to work on her husband's computer, and she fell. I took it to be a father's obligation to remove temptation from her. That is what I did. Upton was a shameless womanizer. I acquainted myself with his habits. Maureen was little more than a target of opportunity for him. He had a different woman every night if he could. The man was an animal. It was because of his habits that I stopped at La Palomba. I was in the parking lot when he drove in. I had my trunk open and called him over to help me get out my spare. When he leaned in, I hit him behind the ear and tumbled him into the trunk. Then I strangled him by twisting jumper cables around his neck. I undressed him down to his silly shorts before closing the trunk. On the way to your rectory, I donated his clothes to St. Vincent de Paul."

"What have you told the police?"

"That I discovered him trying to steal the spare from my trunk. In a rage, I struck him. Harder than I had intended. When I saw that he was dead, I panicked. I lifted him in, closed the trunk, and spent a sleepless night wondering what to do with the body. Of course I had heard of the mob connections with La Palomba. I decided to make it look as if they had done it and put the body in my trunk. At two in the morning, I went outside, opened the trunk, and to my horror found him still alive. I strangled him with the battery jump cable."

"You tell an interesting story."

"The part that must not be told concerns my daughter."

The priest nodded. "You are a ferocious father, Michael O'Halloran."

"I will take that as a compliment."

"The bombing?"

"My own devising. I nearly killed myself in the process, although I had majored in chemistry at St. Francis College. But I wanted to point an unmistakable finger at the mob."

"None of this makes sense, Michael."

"And why not?"

"There was no point in killing Upton. Your daughter had dropped him. Her husband knew nothing."

"Perhaps not. But they had quarreled about what she did all day. I knew that. It was you who convinced me I had best tell the truth."

"I convinced you!"

"If the police investigated Upton's clients, they would be led to Wilhelm. I want to stop that. By some fluke it might come out that he had seduced my daughter. Wilhelm would learn. It would be the end of their marriage."

O'Halloran's wife arrived from Peoria, and the sound of her hysterical crying brought the interview to a close. A woman as short as O'Halloran but weighing twice as much rushed into the room and took the confessed murderer in her arms.

"Is he lying?" Phil Keegan asked.

"About what?"

Phil closed his eyes and breathed through his nose. After a moment he looked at his old friend. "About killing Upton."

"I don't know. What do you think?"

"Guilty or not, I think he is tying a rope around his own neck."

When Father Dowling got home, he had to tell Marie the story, and of course it was the version O'Halloran had given the police.

"Why is he doing it, Father?"

"He says he is guilty."

"Do you believe that?"

"Obviously you don't."

"He is protecting someone, Father. It is the only explanation."

She was too near the truth for comfort. In any case, she was more interested in expressing her own thoughts than in hearing his. She went off, muttering to herself, convinced that anyone with half a brain could see that Michael O'Halloran was making a martyr of himself. Roger Dowling had dreaded that she would mention the daughter, but she did not. Even so, it was a relief to be by himself. Marie had not considered that Michael O'Halloran could be both a murderer and motivated by concern for somebody else.

The next day Cy Horvath phoned. "Father, remember you said O'Halloran's daughter came to see you?"

"Yes."

"What was her name?"

"Maureen."

"She's married, isn't she?"

"You're right."

"And lives in Barrington?"

"She lives in Barrington, yes."

"Is her name Dilthey?"

"Why do you ask?"

"A funny thing. I've been checking out Morton Upton's work record, his clients. Well, he did a job for an outfit in Barrington called Medicure Inc. O'Halloran's son-in-law works for them as an accountant. Upton even made a service call at Dilthey's house."

"So you've connected Upton and O'Halloran after all."

"It looks like it. There's more."

"Oh?"

"We told you about Upton's reputation. A real swinger. Father, he had something going with Maureen Dilthey. That looks like the motive."

"Cy, there's a limit on how much I can discuss this with you. Do you understand?"

There was a thoughtful silence before Cy said, "Priest stuff?"

"Priest stuff."

"Gotcha, Father. Well, I thought you'd want to know what we've found out."

"Thanks, Cy. I do appreciate it."

There was no way the discovery of Maureen's affair with Morton Upton could be kept out of the case against Michael O'Halloran now, as even the little Irishman eventually saw. After a period of rage came resignation, and it was a serene Michael O'Halloran who awaited his trial for the murder of the man who had violated the sanctity of his daughter's home.

"Lieutenant Horvath is a dogged professional, Father Dowling. Despite myself, I admire his tenacity. It was what I dreaded, of course, and why I had to make up that tale for the police. This is hard on Thelma of course." Thelma was Mrs. O'Halloran. "I tell her it will bring us all closer together."

"Let's hope so. You shouldn't have to spend much time in prison."

"Didn't they put Paul in prison, Father?"

"Peter too."

"There you are."

SEVEN

A MONTH LATER when he came back to the rectory from talking to Edna Hospers, director of the parish center, Marie told him both Phil Keegan and Cy Horvath had invited themselves to lunch. They were already at the table when he returned from saying the noon Mass. He stamped snow from his feet, hung up his coat, and joined his guests.

"I didn't see you at Mass," he said.

"We weren't there."

"That explains it."

"Tell him, Cy."

But Lieutenant Horvath was not so easily diverted from the thick vegetable soup Marie had put before him. He finished half the bowl before looking up.

"Remember he said he gave Upton's clothes to St. Vincent de Paul? We found them. After all this time, they were still in the bin. The chapter over in Schaumberg got disorganized and hadn't made any pickups. Just as he said, there were Upton's clothes, his wallet, his ID, everything."

Phil regarded Cy with pride. "So it looks as if he really did do it. I feel a lot better about him going to trial now."

"Did he tell you where the bin was?"

"He even drew a map." Cy fished it out and passed it to Father Dowling. The bin was located in the parking lot of a mall.

"And you found everything?"

Phil said, "How could he know the clothes were there if he didn't put them there?" It was obvious that Phil Keegan still had trouble thinking of Michael O'Halloran as a killer.

Roger Dowling nodded. "Did you take everything from the bin?"

"How do you mean?"

"Were Upton's clothes the only things in the bin?"

"They were what we were after."

That afternoon it began again to snow, and already clogged roads became more treacherous. It was no time to be outside if you could avoid it, and Roger Dowling wavered before pulling on his coat and trudging out to his car. It did not start immediately and he wondered if he would be saved by a weak battery, but then it caught, and he turned on the windshield wipers, which quickly created fans of imperfect visibility. It took him over an hour to get to Schaumburg, and when he turned into the parking lot of the mall, he could see cars having trouble getting traction, spinning their wheels. He left his motor running when he parked beside the bin.

It stood some five feet high and resembled a large mail box. Squinting against the snow, the priest pressed down on the drop and pointed his flashlight into darkness.

"Can we help you, Father?"

Two boys, bundled up in parkas, came toward him. One wore glasses that were opaque with snow; the other had a long yellow scarf wound twice around his neck and still falling to his knees.

"You can indeed. I am trying to retrieve some jumper cables from this box."

"Do you have the key?"

"No, I don't. The only way seems to be to go in after them, and I'm a bit too old for that."

The boy with the scarf volunteered, and after a boost from his companion got a leg over the opening. He let himself down slowly into the bin until only the top of his head showed. Father Dowling handed him the flashlight.

"Do you know what a jumper cable looks like?"

"I'll find it, Father," the small voice echoed from the inside of the bin.

A minute went by, then two. Father Dowling wanted to pray, but he was not sure what his petition should be. Then the boy's face appeared.

"This is the only cable in here, Father."

His mittened hand produced a thick electric cord with odd fittings on either end.

"Is that what you wanted, Father?"

"That's it."

"But it's not a jumper cable."

"I was wrong about that. Can you get out again?"

When the boy with the scarf was out of the bin, helped by his friend, Father Dowling gave each of them a dollar. They said they didn't want anything, but he insisted and watched them hurry across the snowy parking lot to the bright entrance of the mall.

Behind the wheel of his car, he examined the cable. The fitting at one end was a double row of holes, and that at the other had a matching row of pins. He recognized it as belonging to a computer.

He put the car in gear and let it inch forward before applying the gas. Barrington was closer than Fox River. He wondered if Medicure Inc. would still be open when he got there.

MEDICURE INC. was a long low building with a mansard roof, its windows cheerful in the falling snow. The parking lot was filled with cars, most of which were covered with snow, their contours blurred. He parked next to a car that had not been there as long as the others, a familiar car.

Inside was a reception desk and a waiting room, where half a dozen clients sat apprehensively. It was bright and antiseptic and reassuring. The receptionist's hair had the look of meringue and the frames of her glasses sparkled.

"Mr. Dilthey, please."

"In accounting?"

"That's right."

"Won't you have a seat, Father. Someone is with Mr. Dilthey now."

"I know. They're expecting me. How do I get there?"

He followed her directions through swinging double doors and went down a corridor lined with rooms identified by semaphore-like signs that jutted out at right angles to the doors. But accounting was a large open space at the end of the hall, another counter, inside it many desks and, along one wall, a series of enclosed offices. The outer office was obviously nearing the end of the business day. Roger Dowling nodded and smiled as he threaded his way through the desks toward the corner office.

He opened the door and stepped inside. Wilhelm Dilthey sat behind his desk staring up at Cy Horvath. There was a book opened on the desk. The two men turned when the priest entered, but only Dilthey looked surprised. Cy Horvath never looked surprised.

"What brings you here, Father Dowling?" Cy asked.

"This." He put the computer cable on the desk next to the opened book. "I retrieved this from a St. Vincent de Paul bin in Schaumberg."

Dilthey stared at the cable, transfixed, as if it were a deadly serpent. And then he sighed and seemed to sag into his chair.

"We better sit down too," Cy suggested. "Mr. Dilthey and I were discussing Morton Upton's visits here. His most recent visit was on the last day of his life."

"God damn Michael O'Halloran." Dilthey spoke in low measured tones, as if he were indeed uttering a prayer.

"Hasn't he tried to take the blame for something he didn't do?" Roger Dowling asked gently.

"It wouldn't have happened if it weren't for him!"

Cy leaned forward. "What happened, Mr. Dilthey."

"It all started at that damned thirty-fifth wedding anniversary."

THAT SNOWY AFTERNOON in his office at Medicure Inc. was the first time that Wilhelm Dilthey told the convoluted story. In the days and weeks that followed, and six months later at his trial, he would tell it again and again. It incorporated elements of O'Halloran's version. O'Halloran remained a major actor in the tale of what had happened. The irony was that the ferocious father and ferocious Catholic had unwittingly done to his daughter's marriage what he had wished to avert.

Maureen's failure to receive Communion at the anniversary Mass set Michael's mind to work, particularly since Wilhelm Dilthey had approached the altar that day. What in the name of God was his daughter up to? He talked with her and was rebuffed in a sassy manner. Far from putting him off, this fueled his intention to get to the bottom of it, especially now that he suspected the worse.

So it was that he came to know of Morton Upton. What he could not know was that he came in at the end of the affair. During the month when Maureen had resolved to break with Upton, and spent whole days away from the house so that he could not surprise her there, Michael O'Halloran took the fateful step of taking the matter to his son-in-law. Wilhelm became aware that his wife was seldom at home during the day and ultimately accused her of infidelity. It was a typical marital quarrel, not a model of rational exchange, where heated denials are heard as admissions and pleas are taken to be threats. Wilhelm Dilthey resolved to defend his honor in a decisive way. He made an appointment with Morton Upton at Medicure Inc. From there the two men drove to Dilthey's house in order to take a look at an alleged problem with the computer there. Only when they got to the house did Dilthey bring up the subject of his wife. Upton attempted to put it on a man-to-man basis, making light of the adulterous relation. An infuriated Dilthey struck him and strangled him with a computer cable.

He was then confronted with the problem of a dead body. It took him less than ten minutes to decide to share his problem with his father-in-law. Michael O'Halloran drove nonstop from Peoria, and the two men had just gotten the body into the trunk of his car when Maureen returned home.

"I could not fathom their mood, Father. Here were two men who had been willing to stone me, suddenly deferential, almost embarrassed. My father left. Bill went back to the office. Now I know why they acted so strangely."

Now everyone knew. The media covered the story and trial in loving detail. The jury obviously shared the popular view that Wilhelm Dilthey had acted, if not within the law, somehow within his rights. As O'Halloran had hoped, the tragedy did bring the family closer together. The general view was that Dilthey would be paroled in a matter of years. Meanwhile, he was instructing the prisoners at Joliet in computer science.

On a monthly basis, Roger Dowling received a standard mailing from Dasher Development. It served to remind him of the little Irishman whose visit had been the herald of so many improbable events. But he was even less inclined than before to hire professional fund raisers to lift his parish onto a higher financial plateau.

He did not forget to say a Mass for the repose of the soul of Morton Upton. After all, as O'Halloran might have said, Mary Magdalene had been a swinger in her day.

And one day Michael O'Halloran called again. Father Dowling heard the distinctive voice jollying Marie in the hall, and then he appeared in the doorway.

"Father Dowling, you're a sight for sore eyes. And don't look alarmed; I'm not here on business."

O'Halloran accepted a drop of Bushmill's and lifted it in a toast before tossing it off.

"There's something I've been meaning to ask you, Michael."

"Yes, Father."

"Why were you driving around with that body in the trunk of your car."

O'Halloran looked at him for a moment, then winked, leaned forward, and deposited his glass on the desk.

"I applaud you, Father Dowling. Do you know that's a question no one else has put to me."

"What is the answer?"

"Let me say that I was as surprised as you when I opened the trunk and found the body back."

"Back?"

At the La Palomba, having stripped the body, O'Halloran had bundled it into the back seat of the car parked next to his and then gone into his unit. The following morning, having first made certain the other car was gone, he got into his and drove off to St. Hilary's.

"But how did it get back into your trunk?"

"I have a theory about that, Father."

His theory was that he had put the body into a mobster's car, that it had been put back into his trunk when it was discovered, and that in the morning he had been followed to Fox River, where someone let the air out of his tire while he was in the rectory.

Roger Dowling had two choices: either to believe the little fund raiser or disbelieve him. That O'Halloran might have staged the curbside discovery was believable enough. On the other hand, he might be telling the truth. In any case, at this point, it scarcely mattered.

"Now then, should we talk parish finances, Father Dowling?"

In response, the priest called Marie and asked her to give their guest another taste of Irish whiskey.

Heart of Gold

A FATHER DOWLING
MYSTERY NOVELLA

ONE

EDNA HOSPERS, seated at her desk, realized that she had been aware of the sound of shuffling feet in the corridor for some time. She looked up to see old Ray Phillips pass her open door, bent over, head down, as if concentrating on the toes of his shoes. And then he was gone.

Half a minute later he passed the door again, but this time his head was turned toward her. Their eyes met, and immediately Mr. Phillips turned away. Suppressing a smile, Edna rose from her desk and went into the hall. The bent figure shuffled more slowly now, and the angle of his back seemed expectant, as if he awaited something.

"Mr. Phillips," Edna called, and the old man swung around with a feigned look of surprise. "Could you give me a hand in the office, Mr. Phillips?"

"Anything to help."

He stood straighter and walked with less of a shuffle as they went into the office.

This had been going on for a week now, the old man putting in a shy appearance, obviously eager to be of help, but not willing to initiate anything.

What had once been the St. Hilary parish school had long since been turned into a social center by Father Dowling, the pastor, and Edna Hospers had been put in charge. The money enabled her to support herself and her school-age children, but far more important was the sense it gave her of doing something worthwhile. Like old Mr. Phillips, she wanted to be of help.

His bald head reminded her of the plastic hat her son wore when he rode his ten speed, and his brows, permanently raised, lay like circumflex accents on his forehead. Beneath his prominent thin nose was a small white mustache. He had been an accountant in a bank. The first time she asked him to help, he wondered if there was any bookkeeping he might do.

"Oh, I have a very simple system, Mr. Phillips. Father Dowling gives me a set amount for my monthly budget; I have a checking account, and I let the bank keep my records for me."

A small pained look met this remark. "You should always keep independent records, Mrs. Hospers."

"Oh, I'm sure the bank is better at it than I could ever be."

He let it go, but she could see that he disapproved.

"I could ask Father Dowling if he needs your help."

"Oh, I'm sure he must have an accountant already."

"I'll ask." Edna had the feeling the pastor was as little capable as she was to keep an accurate, up-to-date set of books.

Edna went to the noon Mass that day and afterward mentioned Mr. Phillips to Father Dowling.

"Raymond Phillips?"

"Do you know him?"

"Just the name. Ask him to come over to the rectory this afternoon."

The priest had seemed about to say more than that he recognized old Mr. Phillips' name.

"Is he famous or something?"

"He hasn't said anything to you?"

"Only that he wants to help."

"He's been in prison for the past seven years, Edna."

He waited, but she said nothing. Did Father Dowling think Mr. Phillips had been drawn to her because of Gene?

"What prison, Father?"

"Joliet."

Where Gene was. Maybe Mr. Phillips *had* sought her out. Good Lord, had he known Gene in prison? Edna felt the blush spread over her face. After all this time, she still could not accept the fact that she was the wife of a convict. Father Dowling put a hand on her arm.

"About two? Why don't you come with him, Edna? That will be easier than giving him directions."

That was so like Father Dowling, quick to notice, quick to help. Even Gene had said that the pastor of St. Hilary could give religion a good name.

A car had pulled into the curb, and Captain Phil Keegan got out of it and walked toward them. No doubt he had come to have lunch with Father Dowling. Edna still felt resentment at the role Keegan had played in her husband's conviction, which didn't make a lot of sense, maybe, but she felt it nonetheless. The pastor of St. Hilary's had been more responsible than the Fox River captain of detectives for Gene's arrest.

"I'll bring him, Father."

Back in her office, having her sandwich and a Diet Coke, Edna took comfort from the fact that she had never suspected Mr. Phillips was a former prisoner. He had mentioned working in a bank when she asked him what he had done, and she assumed he had left the job on reaching retirement age. Were there telltale signs of those seven years? She didn't think so. That he had his odd mannerisms did not distinguish him from the rest of the old people who came each day to the school. Few offered to help with the work, but then that is not why they came. The main reason was to have someone to be with, to talk to, play cards with, not feel completely on the shelf. If Mr. Phillips felt better keeping busy, that was fine with Edna. But now her curiosity about the old man dramatically increased. After eating only half her sandwich, she went in search of Raymond Phillips.

He wasn't in the lunchroom, he wasn't in the library, and he wasn't in the gym, where shuffleboard and bridge and, rarely, volleyball were played.

"Is that old billiard ball's name?" Joe Plaisance said when she stopped at the bridge table, where he was currently dummy.

"Why do you call him that?" Edna asked angrily.

Bob McDonald answered, not looking up from his hand. "Haven't you ever seen him with his hat off? He looks like Yul Brynner."

"While he was still alive," Joe added, and the other three at the table laughed.

Edna was furious with them. She turned on her heel and hurried out of the gym. Why did they make fun of Mr. Phillips? Did they know what she had only just now learned from Father Dowling? She could have cried at the unfairness of it. The poor man. Seven years in prison, and now they made jokes about him.

But Edna knew that her anger was caused in large part because it might have been Gene they were making fun of. She wished she had not passed Mr. Phillips on to Father Dowling. If she had known of his past, would she have told the pastor? Edna now felt especially protective of Raymond Phillips.

When she got back to her office after the noon Mass, the old man was waiting for her, smiling sheepishly.

"Notice anything different?"

Edna circled him, looking closely, but he seemed unchanged to her. His smile broadened.

"On your desk."

It was a wooden statue, ten inches high, a saint carrying a child. She didn't know what to say.

"St. Anthony of Padua," he explained. "I made it in prison."

"Joliet?"

"Yes."

She looked at him. Did he expect her to mention Gene? She felt it was a secret they already shared.

He said, "You lose anything, ask St. Anthony. He never fails."

It seemed an odd endorsement from a man who had spent years in prison.

"I can't take it from you, Mr. Phillips."

"Think of it as a donation. To the parish."

Edna went to him and kissed the top of his head. There were tears in her eyes when she turned away.

She moved the statue to the back of her desk. It was heavier than it looked, and she was about to ask Mr. Phillips what kind of wood it was made of, but he had slipped away.

TWO

"I'M SURPRISED he came back to the old neighborhood," Phil Keegan said, wiping his lips with his napkin. "Marie," he called toward the kitchen, "that was wonderful minestrone."

"Minestrone!" came the disgusted reply. "That is just plain vegetable soup."

"Nothing plain about it."

Roger Dowling pushed back from the table, preferring to continue their conversation in his study. There was no need to shout for Marie Murkin to pick up every word spoken at the dining-room table. She eavesdropped in the line of duty, maintaining that as housekeeper she should always know what was going on—short of matters of conscience, of course.

"Do you mind, Roger?" Phil asked, flourishing an enormous cigar as he settled down.

"Where on earth did you get that?"

"Liberati's wife had twins."

"He should have given you two cigars. Go ahead. Light it. What did you mean about Raymond Phillips returning to his old neighborhood?"

"I told you all about him a few weeks ago when he got out."

"Refresh my memory." The first time Roger Dowling had paid only imperfect attention. Nevertheless, the name had registered as soon as Edna said it; he knew he had heard it before, remembered being told that Phillips had spent seven years in Joliet. This time he paid full attention to Phil's story and pressed for further details.

Raymond Phillips had lived in the neighborhood long before Roger Dowling had been assigned to St. Hilary's. What was apparent exile, the dashing of all hope of clerical advancement, became the best thing that had happened to him in a quarter of a century as a priest. Phil Keegan, an old friend, veteran of the Fox River police department and a widower, was a frequent presence in the rectory, always a fund of information. In fifteen minutes Roger Dowling knew essentially all that Keegan did about Raymond Phillips.

His crime had been embezzlement. Over a period of years, he had skimmed small amounts from a random series of accounts. He had not been greedy and he had been more than careful. It was estimated that before he was done he had stolen approximately fifty thousand dollars.

"Approximately?"

"Roger, my story is just beginning."

Father Dowling glanced at his watch. In twenty minutes, Edna Hospers was due to bring Phillips to the rectory. "How was the embezzlement discovered?"

"It wasn't. It might never have been if he hadn't reported it."

"What prompted him to do that?"

Phil laughed, watching rich steel-blue smoke rise among the bookshelves in the study. "He was robbed. Somebody broke into his house and made off with the cookie tin in which he kept the fifty thousand."

This might have been considered an ingenious ploy if it had not been for Phillips's condition. He had been at home at the time of the break-in and had been severely beaten by the thief. The prosecutor would suggest that Phillips' bruises were self-inflicted, but the accountant insisted he had seen the man and was more than willing to identify him. It was then that he revealed that he had embezzled fifty thousand dollars. He was prosecuted, found guilty, and given thirty years.

Keegan shook his head. "Fifty thousand dollars! Brazil can welsh on paying *interest* on fifty billion and the banks swallow it, but Phillips was an employee, and they didn't want it to look like their bank was full of embezzlers."

"You make it sound as if the bank, not the prosecutor, took him to court."

"They both did. The bank got everything he had as well as their money back. They took his house, his furniture, his car, everything."

"So he made restitution?"

"With interest. Unlike Mexico, Brazil, you name it."

Phil seemed to have an impressionistic understanding of international finance, but Roger got his point.

"At least he didn't have to serve the whole sentence, Phil."

Keegan sat forward, frowning. "He's dying, Roger. Leukemia. Maybe they wanted to save the state the price of the funeral."

It was not simply Phillips's mortal illness that explained Keegan's uncharacteristic sympathy for the criminal. "Think of it, Roger. Sure he took the money, but he didn't spend it. He said he never spent a dime of it, and I believe him. In effect, what he did was become an annex to the bank, a home savings institution. Nobody was even inconvenienced. People were paid their interest, drew on their accounts, nothing Phillips did really mattered. And as I said, the bank got its money back. You could say that Phillips was the victim of a bank robbery rather than a bank robber."

Equally in Phillips' favor was the exemplary family he had raised. Three daughters, two sons.

"One of the daughters was a nun."

"Was? Did she leave?"

"She died." Keegan took a scissors from the desk and cut off the burning end of his cigar. "Of leukemia."

EDNA HOSPERS ARRIVED at a quarter of two while Phil Keegan was still there. She rang the front door bell, burst through the door, and came running down the hall to stand breathless in the open door of the study.

"He's gone! Father, they've taken him away." She looked wildly from the priest to the detective. "Kidnapped!"

Roger Dowling was on his feet. He took Edna's elbow and led her to a chair. She collapsed in it, sobbing.

"After everything else that's happened to him, now this."

"Raymond Phillips," the priest explained to Keegan.

Keegan too had stood. Now he knelt in front of Edna, took her hands, and then slammed them down on the upholstered arms of the chair.

"Quit the blubbering! Tell me exactly what happened. Stop the bawling!"

She did. But not before an open-mouthed Marie Murkin arrived on the scene. She seemed torn between indignation that anyone, even Edna, had just burst into the house and anger at Keegan's tone. She bustled into the study and claimed one of Edna's hands from Phil Keegan. Edna Hospers, her hands being held by two adults, might have been a child telling of Raymond Phillips' disappearance from the parish school.

Kidnapping seemed an exaggeration for what had happened. But then Edna's emotions and imagination were engaged because of Phillips' imprisonment. Two men had come asking for Mr. Phillips, and he had been seen talking with them in the playground. It was Joe Plaisance who saw them push Mr. Phillips into the car and drive away with him. The expression on Phil's face made clear what he thought of the tale.

"We'll look into it," he said, getting to his feet.

Edna stared up at him in disbelief. "You'll look into it! That's what I tell my kids when I mean no. We'll see." She looked at Marie Murkin, who sought her clue from Roger Dowling. "Father, I am serious. They forced him into that car and took him away."

In the doorway of the study now, Phil said, "I'll go over and talk to the witness." He could not keep sarcasm from his voice. "Joe Plaisance is his name?"

"Joe Plaisance is his name," Edna repeated icily. "And please treat him as you would any other adult."

"You come with me, Edna," Marie said. "I'll make you a cup of tea."

"They'll find out what happened, Edna," Roger Dowling assured her.

She turned on her way out of the study.' "I know what happened, Father." And she went on to the kitchen with Marie Murkin.

JOE PLAISANCE'S NAME was familiar to Keegan because Plaisance was a retired Fox River policeman. "Not much of a cop," he told Roger later, but some elements of training are never lost. Plaisance had noted both the make of the automobile in which Phillips had been taken as well as its license plate.

"Indiana." Keegan took out the cigar he had begun earlier, but after a loving consideration of it he returned it to his pocket. "Phillips has relatives in Indiana. One of his sons lives in Plymouth, Roger."

"Where is that?"

"Below South Bend." South Bend was a familiar point of reference. They tried to see at least one Notre Dame home game each fall.

"Below in what sense?"

"South of. The plate indicates that area."

"Just taking Grandpa home for a visit, is that your idea?"

"Until something better comes along."

"Did Plaisance say the old man was forced into the car?"

"Sure he did. Until I asked him what he meant by that. They might have been giving him a hand is all."

"I hope you'll keep me posted, Phil."

Keegan looked at him with a half-forced smile. "Sure. Because it happened here. You have a right to know. But don't hold your breath."

Roger Dowling went over to the school to tell Edna what had been learned, but she had already heard.

"Joe Plaisance can't see across the gymnasium."

"He noted the license plate, didn't he?"

"Laura Zimmer read it to him. If she hadn't been there, Joe Plaisance would not have provided the police with an excuse to ignore what happened."

"Did they talk to Laura?"

"I doubt it."

Laura Zimmer, blue hair, blue-rimmed plastic spectacles, her lips set in the whistling position, was frowning over a game of solitaire in a corner of the gym. Roger Dowling spoke her name, and she answered, "What?" before looking up, and then when she saw who it was she got quite flustered. She tried to get up but the cast on her foot made that impossible. Roger Dowling pulled up a chair. "Tell me about the men who took away Mr. Phillips."

Her lips became a pout. "Maybe you should ask Joseph Plaisance, Father. He is the famous eyewitness. Why, he is a regular owl."

"Edna tells me you were the one who really saw it."

"I don't consider it an accomplishment, Father Dowling. The fact is I was sitting by the window feeling sorry for myself when I looked out and saw it. Joe was at a nearby bridge table, and I called him over. But he is perfectly welcome to all the fame and glory."

"Maybe he'll split the reward."

"Reward!"

Then she saw that he was teasing her. She nodded and looked sad. "One of the most trying things about growing old is that one begins to act like a child again."

"Some of us don't wait until we're old."

"You probably mean that in some religious sense."

"Good heavens, no." It was his turn to feel foolish. *Unless you become as little children.* Is that what she thought he meant? It was painful to think she would expect such unctuousness from him. "Tell me what happened, Laura."

Her story was unequivocal. Two men had practically dragged poor old Mr. Phillips to a car they had first driven onto the playground. "What he was doing out there on a day like this is hard to say. The wind was like ice, and he wore only that argyle coat sweater he has worn every day he's been here."

"Have you gotten to know him at all, Laura?"

"He was shy as a bird. When I'm in that" —she nodded at her wheelchair— "I can get around all right, but I can't stand sitting in it all the time. Can't stand sitting," she repeated and shook her head. She had taught sixth grade in the Fox River public school system for forty-three years. "If I called him over, he would always look around to see if I really meant him. He never thought anyone wanted to talk to him."

"But you did talk?"

"Do you know his story, Father?"

"Yes."

"Isn't it sad? To be branded a thief and have everything stolen from you and still spend all that time in prison. Prison sounds worse than Dante's *Inferno,* Father Dowling. His children never came to see him in all those years. He has a dozen grandchildren he has never seen, and he only knows of them because of Beth. She's his granddaughter too. She lives in River Forest."

"She visited him in prison?"

"She wrote to him. He didn't really want anyone to see him there. Do you know how he refers to himself? As the penitent. His idea is that he has to make up for what he has done, and he doesn't want to burden the family with it." She sniffed. "As if they cared."

"How can I get in touch with Beth?"

Laura unsnapped a purse the size of an overnight bag and took from it a slip of paper. She flourished it. "He gave me this. Her address. I've written the phone number below."

"Where did you get the phone number?"

"I looked it up. She hasn't answered yet, but I suppose she's working. She's an architect. Just twenty-three years old and already an architect. Mr. Phillips was very proud of that. It is so cruel that he thinks it almost presumptuous of him to feel proud of his family."

"Maybe the Indiana branch decided to get in touch with him?"

"By wrestling him into a car? I don't mean any offense, Father. I have a hunch that Beth will know what to do. Heaven knows we can't depend on the police."

"Do you mind if I telephone Beth?"

Pale blue eyes regarded him from the blue frames of her glasses. Did she think that he, like Joe Plaisance, meant to usurp her role?

He said, "I'll ask if she can come here, and if she does I'll want you there when I talk to her. Does she know you're a friend of her grandfather's?"

"I don't want to make it sound like more than it was, Father."

"Of course not."

Another of the oddities of the old was the romantic crushes they developed. Tottering old ladies became giggling school girls, and frail old men began metaphorically to thump their chests and huff and puff. It appeared that Laura Zimmer had such a romantic interest in the egg-bald accountant who had been forced into a car that afternoon.

Kidnapping no longer seemed too strong a word, and Roger Dowling told Edna Hospers that.

"Of course he was kidnapped. I'm glad you don't agree with Captain Keegan."

"I don't think Laura would exaggerate."

The chill that had been there between them earlier was gone now, and Edna was delighted to hear of the granddaughter Beth. Roger Dowling tried to get through to the young woman from the phone in Edna's office, not because he thought she would be home at this hour—it was not yet four—but as a further peace offering.

In any event, he did not have to make the call. Beth showed up on his doorstep that evening.

THREE

HER BLOND HAIR FELL over her forehead in such a way that Father Dowling had the uneasy sense of being peered at through foliage by a woodland nymph. How could she see anything but her own hair?

"You're Father Dowling? I'm Beth." She lifted her chin. "Raymond Phillips is my grandfather."

"Have you heard what happened to him?"

"That's why I'm here."

He took her into a front parlor after asking Marie Murkin to bring hot cocoa for their guest.

"Hot cocoa!"

"Don't you like it?" Roger Dowling asked sympathetically.

"I love it. Do you have marshmallows too?"

Even Marie was caught up in the young woman's enthusiasm, though she felt constrained to say that the cocoa came in packets and all she did was add hot water. But Beth would not let her delight be diminished.

When Marie was gone, Beth became subdued. "I parked near what I suppose is the school. That's where it happened, isn't it?"

"It?"

"The kidnapping."

"Have you talked with Laura Zimmer?"

Her nod redistributed the hair on her forehead. She had slipped out of her raincoat, brushed aside his offer to hang it up, and sat across the table from him.

"She insisted I come see you."

"Did she tell you about the license plate?"

"It doesn't surprise me a bit. That would have been my guess even if she hadn't noticed the Indiana license. It was my uncles, Maurice, and Steve, I'm sure of it. The car belongs to Steve."

"Then the police will trace it to him. Have you thought of going to Indiana to be with your grandfather?"

"If I thought it would help, I would."

"How do you mean?"

"My grandfather is a tough old guy. The things he's been through in his life. You know he was in prison for years."

"Did he talk of that much?"

"Almost never. That's how bad it was. Imagine paying for a crime you didn't commit."

"Didn't he confess to embezzlement?"

"He admitted taking money from the bank."

Father Dowling waited, but she did not go on. Apparently she thought she had made an important distinction.

"You don't think he was guilty?"

"He took the money from the bank and kept it in his house, Father. He kept it at his home. He couldn't decide whether he meant to keep it or return it. If he had decided to keep it, that would have been embezzlement. But he still hadn't decided when someone stole the money from him."

"As I understand the story, he never even ventured a guess who the thief might be."

"Did you talk with him about it, Father?"

Once more Roger Dowling was embarrassed that he had not gotten to know Raymond Phillips, although the old man had been coming to St. Hilary's for weeks. "I'm afraid most of my information is at third hand."

"He doesn't know who stole the money, and he won't guess."

"But you think he knows?"

"Sure."

"Did he tell you?"

"He didn't have to. I think it's why we got along so well. It was my father who took it."

"Your father! Did your grandfather tell you that?"

"As I said, he didn't have to."

Beth's father had failed at everything he had undertaken. From his daughter's description of him, he had been a born entrepreneur, one project scarcely begun before he was overwhelmed by another irresistible idea.

"And they were good ideas, Father. His note-books were full of them. Sometimes he would write pages, very quickly, ideas for products just tumbling one after the other. His problem was always capital."

He would start on a shoestring, soon become overextended, borrow at high rates, and go under. By then he was usually in the grips of another idea and was not dismayed to fail. Most of his ideas had to do with uses of the computer, and Roger Dowling could not follow Beth's explanation. At the time of the theft, her father was on the threshold of a heady success. He had acquired the rights to two German, one French, one Italian, and one Spanish encyclopedias.

The idea was to provide these on-line to research libraries. He had signed up several dozen libraries, he had the rights to the encyclopedias, he had hired a crew to enter the data into the computer along with an original way to gain access to the data. He was at a point where a determinate amount of cash, forty thousand dollars, was the difference between his first big success and folding ignominiously again, this time with the promised land in sight.

She was interrupted by the arrival of Marie with the cocoa, and once more her almost childish delight at the prospect of hot cocoa with marshmallows afloat in it seemed to light up the room. She actually got up and kissed Marie Murkin who withdrew in confusion.

"I gather your father did not fail."

She licked her lips. "Oh eventually, yes. But he survived the forty thousand dollar crisis. One day it was all I heard at home, the next it was not mentioned. But he failed, all right. Seven months later. Library budgets were slashed, more than half his clients withdrew, and after a few frantic weeks it was all over."

Roger Dowling had let Marie bring him cocoa too. Cocoa was part of her campaign to get him to drink less coffee. She had resolved that after supper he would get no more coffee, at least served by her. He didn't like cocoa, or so he had thought. The infectious Beth made him want to try it at least. He liked it. Of course he could never admit that to Marie Murkin.

Beth's father was now living in Pamplona, far from the reach of his creditors. She had spoken with him an hour ago— "Of course it's quite late at night there." —to tell him what had happened to his father.

"What did he say?"

"Maurice and Steve."

"But why?"

"Well, of course my father can't say why, but I can. They don't believe the money was ever stolen. They think he still has fifty thousand dollars, and that now it is his."

"They think he spent all those years in prison, lost everything he had, including it seems his family, for fifty thousand dollars?"

"Do you mean it doesn't sound like enough money? I can't imagine any amount being enough."

"But your uncles can."

She made a face. "What about the other side of it, Father. Speaking as a priest. Would the money now be his?"

It was the kind of problem posed in moral theology classes when he was in the seminary. If Raymond Phillips had repaid the money and the interest it would have earned in the bank with money raised by selling his house and other property, and if he had spent all those years in prison while retaining the fifty thousand dollars he had stolen, wasn't *that* fifty thousand rightfully his? If not his, whose? To give it to the bank would be a donation. Roger Dowling knew that some rigorists would hold that he should not profit from his wrong deed, but if the profit was outbalanced many times by what he had paid, it seemed that the fifty thousand dollars had to be his. Think of it as the value of his house and property, rather than the money taken from the bank, and it was not the fruit of his embezzlement.

"Of course, if your father stole it, that's a moot point."

"But what if he hadn't?"

Why did he hesitate to give her the answer he thought was just? Let Raymond Phillips keep the money; it was his. Beth was peering at him, obviously wanting an answer.

"Next you'll want me to agree that he didn't steal it."

"I don't think he did. I don't think it was stealing."

"Do you think he'll convince your uncles he doesn't have the money?"

"I wonder if they'll be able to convince the police they shouldn't be arrested for kidnapping Grandfather."

When Beth got up to go, he told her to come by again any time, for cocoa. "I'll be expecting to see your grandfather back again too, and this time we will take better care of him."

"Oh, Father, please don't think I'm criticizing you."

She said it as if she often had to assure people she wasn't criticizing. There was a kind of innocent accusativeness in her manner, as if the world were failing to meet up to her high standards. Father Dowling himself felt half under indictment while speaking with Beth. If it had not been for her delight in the cocoa, he might have been tempted to tell her that her quarrel was with her relatives, not with him.

PHIL KEEGAN STOPPED BY to watch a Bulls game being played on the West Coast. Only after the first quarter did he mention the Indiana Phillips.

"They claim they were at home all day and all night and that the car whose license plate we were tracing was in the garage getting a tune up." Phil tipped his head back as he drained his bottle of beer.

"Is it true?"

"The garage backs them up."

"That doesn't seem to convince you."

"The garage is run by the son of Steven Phillips."

"What an incestuous family—so to speak."

Phil frowned away the implications of the word, and Roger Dowling was sorry he had used it. Phil was a great family man, although he was a widower whose two daughters lived at opposite ends of the country, and he did not take lightly any reminder that sometimes the sacred family bond was sinned against.

"It does go around in circles," he agreed when he returned from the kitchen with a fresh bottle of beer.

Indeed it does, Roger Dowling mused, as he settled back to watch the graceful flow of the game. Raymond Phillips embezzles fifty thousand dollars, which is then stolen by his son, whereupon the embezzler selflessly goes to prison, presumably to protect the family honor. Now, having paid his debt, he is kidnapped by two other sons because they think he still has the money, an action that disgusts the granddaughter Beth. However, an alibi is provided the Indiana Phillips by Beth's cousin, who claims he was giving a tune up to the car that Laura Zimmer, a reliable eyewitness, says was at the time in Fox River, the very vehicle in which from a window of St. Hilary's school she saw Raymond Phillips taken away against his will. If not incestuous, these events were certainly all in the family.

The whole complexion of these events changed when, in the game's third quarter, the telephone rang. Roger Dowling handed the phone to the reluctant Keegan, who kept his eyes on the screen, where the Bulls were trailing by 12.

A moment after putting the phone to his ear, Phil was on his feet. He looked down at Roger Dowling.

"A body thought to be Raymond Phillips' is at the morgue. Would you come make an identification?"

Roger Dowling rose, saddened by the thought that all he could do for the old man now was identify him. Of course that was not true. He breathed a prayer for Raymond Phillips as they went out to the car.

FOUR

THE BODY WAS INDEED that of Raymond Phillips. Roger Dowling's identification sufficed; there was no need to call a member of the family, at least for that purpose. He felt that he had done Beth a favor. It would be easier for her to see the body later, at a mortuary, prepared for viewing, lying in state among the flowers. To see the old man now, a shriveled lifeless body, a cold corpse in a cold morgue, was to look on the unadorned face of death.

"They picked seven slugs out of the body, Roger. It has the marks of a gangland killing."

"Fellow alumni from Joliet?"

"Maybe. The question is why. He would have had to irritate somebody very much to be killed like that."

The body had been found in the front seat of a rusting wheelless Plymouth in a junkyard that overlooked the Fox River below the town. The old man's hands had been tied behind his back, and there were signs he had been beaten severely before being shot.

"Maybe he wouldn't tell them what they wanted to hear."

"Like what?"

"Where the money is he stole from the bank."

Phil, lighting a cigar, squinted at Roger Dowling through the smoke. "But the bank money was stolen from him."

"Maybe they don't believe that."

Phil thought a moment, then shook his head. "Wouldn't that be something, after all these years, still to be paying for that old crime? They would have to be very stupid to think he still had that money. Why would he go to prison rather than produce it?"

"Everything he owned was lost, wasn't it?"

"That got him no leniency from the court. But if he had produced the money and paid the interest, he could have gotten away with a nominal sentence." Phil shook his head. "Naw. Only an idiot would think he would take a long sentence for the money."

Idiots of the kind Beth had taken her uncles to be? Phil said he would send Cy Horvath down to Joliet to see if he could get a lead. Meanwhile, they would go tell Beth Phillips the sad news.

BETH HAD NOT STRUCK Roger Dowling as a swooning female, but at the news of her grandfather's death, she literally fainted. Roger Dowling was glad that Phil Keegan was with him. Ironically, on the way from the car to Beth's door, he had said, "If I know this girl, Phil, she will take it pretty well."

Which meant that he did not know Beth. Phil picked her up and carried her across the studio apartment to the couch, where he draped her in a half-seated, half-lying position. And then slapped her face.

The blow shocked Roger Dowling, but Beth's eyes fluttered open and she looked around as if her own apartment was new to her. At the sight of Roger Dowling, her hand went to her mouth but not in time to suppress a sob.

"Raymond Philips is dead, Miss," Phil Keegan said in no-nonsense tones. "Father Dowling identified the body."

Roger found a glass and brought water, but Beth was by now resuming the character he had assumed was hers. She took the water and drank, but it was more a concession to his thoughtfulness than from any need for its restorative effects.

"Give me the details," she said, addressing Phil.

"He was found dead in an abandoned car in the ABC Junkyard."

Her lip quivered, but she willed herself to remain in control.

"He had been shot seven times."

"Oh my God."

She sat through the grim details without further sign of weakness but also, Roger Dowling noticed, without comment. He also noticed that neither Phil nor the granddaughter seemed to recall that the murdered man had been thought to be in Indiana unwillingly in the custody of his sons.

It was forty-five minutes later when they left the apartment, and it was clear that Phil wanted to stop by the rectory for a nightcap. That the pastor no longer drank did not affect Phil's enjoyment of a beer in his company. Marie Murkin was still up, and Phil told her about Raymond Phillips.

"I knew something bad was going to happen to that man," Marie declared, but she was not a prophetess who took pleasure in the accuracy of her intuitions.

"Why so?" Phil unwisely asked, even though he tried to keep his tone disinterested.

"The way Edna worried about him."

Neither man felt inclined to ask what that meant. It was preferable to go over the details of how the body was found and the fact that Phillips had been shot.

"The Phillipses were always strange," Marie said. "Do you suppose he still had that money?"

"Oh sure," Phil said. "He probably put it in the bank just before going off to prison for stealing it." He snorted. "Marie, he could have saved more than that during those years if he had not been in prison."

"Then who stole it?"

Phil never liked being reminded of unsolved crimes, and nothing was less likely to attract him than appeal to an unknown thief to explain the missing money. But Raymond Phillip's years in prison could not be ignored, and they seemed sufficient corroboration of his story that the embezzled money had been stolen from him in turn.

"Then why would anyone kill him now?" Marie asked.

"For the money," Roger Dowling said.

"There?"

"Not because he had it, Marie. It was only necessary that someone thought he had it."

"And who might that be?"

"Anyone," Phil Keegan growled.

Marie tipped her head to the side and looked at him. "I'm only trying to help, Captain."

"This is delicious cocoa, Marie," Roger Dowling said, and Marie turned to him angrily.

"You don't have to drink it if you don't want to."

"I'd like some if there's more," Phil said.

It seemed an unhappy combination, but Phil followed his beer with cocoa.

After Marie went off to her apartment above the kitchen, Phil said, "Roger, don't encourage anyone to think Phillips still had that money."

"I wonder where it went."

"Please, Roger, not while I'm drinking cocoa."

"Have another beer."

But Phil got up to go. "I want to get an early start in the morning."

Roger Dowling sat on in his study, puffing on his pipe, trying to get the cloying taste of marshmallow from his mouth, wondering what he might do to be of help to Phil. He felt little inclination to go to bed. An old man dying of leukemia, killed in a cruel way for money he did not have. It seemed a profound allegory of human life, but doubtless that was because of the lateness of the hour.

FIVE

IF CY THOUGHT it was a wild-goose chase he didn't let
on, but after the lieutenant had set off for Joliet the
following day, Keegan sat in his office musing over
the fate of Raymond Phillips. Why he had stolen the
money in the first place was the hardest thing to understand. Had he dreamt of early retirement, going
off somewhere with his wife where he could live beyond the limits of his pension and social security
without attracting attention? Well, his wife had died
a year before Phillips startled the town by announc-
ing that he had been robbed of the fifty thousand
dollars he had embezzled from the bank, where he
was a trusted employee. On Keegan's desk were the
reports made at the time. Phillips's house gave every
evidence of having been ransacked. Drawers had been
emptied, the attic and basement torn apart, the clos-
ets rid of their contents. It might have been worse, but
apparently the money had been discovered before the
house was completely dismantled. Phillips claimed
the money was hidden in a cookie tin buried in a hole
beneath the back porch. The tin and the hole were
there, but the money was gone. If there had been any

money. That skepticism about the missing money had prompted Phillips to bring up the embezzlement.

Why did he mention it? Why did he report the theft, for that matter? It was bad enough to have stolen the money, but after it was stolen from him, Phillips could have cut his losses by remaining silent. Either he had feared the embezzlement would be discovered anyway—unlikely, since without Phillips the auditors would never have discovered it—or that the thief would blow the whistle on him. But that meant the thief knew Phillips was an embezzler. Had his colleagues at the bank been questioned?

Extensively, the records showed. Keegan felt a sense of pride as he reviewed the investigation. After all this time and under no pressure, he still could not think of anything that might have been done that had not been done. By contrast, sending Cy to Joliet seemed about as rational as expecting to win at Lotto. Nonetheless, Cy's phone call seemed to provide justification for the trip.

"No one here is of any help, Captain, but he had a cell mate for several years who was also released. A man named Martin."

"Dwayne Martin?"

"I thought you might remember him."

"We should have his address."

It was of course a Fox River address, since the paroled Martin had to return to the city where he had been convicted. Keegan decided to call on Martin himself.

Dwayne Martin's criminal career had been based on the automobile. Perhaps in an earlier time he would have been a horse thief, but in the twentieth century his specialty was inevitably cars. He stole them, drove them for others who were committing crimes, sold them. He had been involved with a chop shop; he had been suspected of driving for the mob but never convicted of it before the aborted attempt on the Lincoln Savings and Loan in Fox River. Ten minutes after the two men in the bank had been taken into custody, Dwayne still waited dutifully behind the wheel of the stolen Mercedes in which he was meant to drive the thieves and money away. During his questioning, Dwayne had insistently put a question of his own. Had the guys in the bank fingered him? The answer was no, but Dwayne Martin never had the satisfaction of being told that.

"He's teaching school today," said the woman behind the desk of the residence hotel in which Dwayne Martin lived.

"Dwayne Martin is teaching?"

"Lecturing," she said, speaking through the bridge of her nose.

"In a school?"

"Grover Cleveland."

Dwayne Martin, wearing a maroon sport coat and a white woolen turtleneck, was speaking to a civics class, telling them a life of crime was pointless.

"Walk away from temptation," he was saying in a scrappy voice. "Say no to crime."

"Say hello to me," Phil suggested when the bell had rung and Miss Simmons, the teacher, was thanking Dwayne profusely for bringing this needed message to her class.

"But when I think of their home conditions..." Her eyes rolled heavenward.

"What the hell are you doing here, Keegan?"

"Let's talk."

"Who is this man?" Miss Simmons demanded, sensing trouble.

Keegan showed her his ID and explained that he wished to consult with Mr. Martin. The *Mr.* and the verb *consult* allayed her fears. Keegan and Martin threaded their way down a noisy corridor lined with lockers and teeming with kids.

"What's it about?" Martin asked when they were outside. Keegan stood in the weak sunlight on the school steps and relit his cigar.

"Raymond Phillips."

"I knew him in Joliet. Something happen to him?"

"He's in the morgue."

Martin said nothing for a time, studying Keegan closely for clues. "I knew he was sick."

"He was shot seven times. Generally that has the effect of making someone dead, especially if he has been knocked around first."

Martin turned his head but kept his eyes on Keegan. "Naw. Not Ray. Who would want to hurt Ray?"

"That's the question I want you to give me an answer to, Dwayne. Ever hear of the ABC Junkyard?"

"I work there."

"When you're not teaching."

"Why the hell are you leaning on me, Keegan?"

"Phillips's body was found in one of the cars in the junkyard by a mechanic scrounging for spare parts."

Keegan realized he had seen that expression on Dwayne Martin's face before. It was the way he had looked when he asked if his friends had betrayed him.

"Why are they doing this to you, Dwayne?"

It was the right question. Dwayne Martin was more than willing to talk about his old cell mate. Keegan didn't take him to his office. They stopped off for a beer in the bar across from the courthouse, and it was there, in a booth, that Dwayne told his story.

"What made you think Phillips still had the money, Dwayne? Did he tell you that?"

"Flat-out no. But that's what he was saying. I used to kid him about the time he would have when he got out, and he would smile and smile."

"Did you ever look him up?"

"I meant to. He was a nice man. I talked about him and said he and I would get together some day." Dwayne passed his hand over his narrow face and looked bleakly around the bar. "I should have known."

He had told fellow workers of the little embezzler he had met in Joliet, a guy with at least fifty thousand dollars in cash hidden away, free and clear, when he got out.

"I might just as well have taken out a contract on him."

"I want the names, Dwayne."

"You're damn right I'll give you the names."

SIX

LAURA ZIMMER had maneuvered her wheelchair into a room that was still set up like a classroom. Here it was that Roger Dowling gave catechism lessons to children of the parish who attended the public school. Now he cleared his throat in the doorway, the classic signal to announce one's presence, but Laura continued to look out the window. The priest crossed the room and sat on a desk top a few feet from her. Laura turned to him with an abject expression on her face.

"You've heard about Raymond Phillips?"

She nodded. "It's just an item of news here, Father, part of the daily gossip."

She was referring to the other old people.

"The others didn't know him very well."

"Neither did I!"

"But better than most."

"I suppose."

The priest took out his pipe, palming the bowl, but it was like holding a gun, so he put it unlit in his mouth. "It was a cruel way to die."

"And without dignity. They found him in a junk-yard!"

"Yes."

"And shot. What kind of people he must have lived with all those years."

"There may be a connection there at that. I just had a call from Captain Keegan. They've arrested two men."

"Why would they kill him, Father Dowling?"

"You must have given that some thought yourself."

She looked alarmed and turned again to the window.

"Do you think they were the kidnappers, Laura?"

She said nothing, just snuffled into the Kleenex she had taken from her sweater pocket.

The priest said, "What I can't understand is the Indiana license plate. Why would anyone come all the way from Indiana to kill an old man?"

She spun her chair around to face him, and her eyes sparkled through the tears. "There weren't any kidnappers, Father Dowling. That was just a story."

He nodded, saying nothing.

"And I didn't see an Indiana license. All I saw was the two men push him into the car."

"Then he was actually taken away in a car?"

"Father, I only said those things to help. The idea was to get him out of the reach of his relatives."

"While making it look as if they had taken him away."

"Yes."

"And Beth gave you the plate number, the one you said you saw?"

"I had no idea anything like this could happen. It was supposed to be imaginary, and then it became real. He was kidnapped. Good Lord, Father, that poor old man shot again and again and then left like that." She squeezed her eyes shut as if to ward off the painful image.

"Was the plan that Beth would take her grandfather away?"

She looked beseechingly at him. "I would rather you put these questions to her, Father. I can only answer for myself, and I have never felt worse in my life."

HE CALLED and invited Beth to lunch, and it was pretty obvious that she did not want to face him.

"Did Laura come see you, Father?"

"I went to her."

"So you know."

"Beth, who will be in charge of arrangements for your grandfather's funeral?"

"I will!"

He might have known that the opportunity to do something for her grandfather, even now when it was too late, would be irresistible to her. They arranged to meet at McDivitt's Funeral Home at ten the following morning, and Beth entered into the gruesome arrangements with a gusto that took old McDivitt by surprise. The undertaker had a practiced patter with which he urged the bereaved into as lavish a send-off as he could, suggesting they owed it to the dear departed, but Beth was well ahead of him, insisting on the most expensive casket, agreeing that they would need at least two cars beside the hearse. McDivitt's scalp glowed pinkly through his sparse and cottony hair, but he managed not to rub his hands. Father Dowling decided it would be unwise to suggest moderation to Beth. An elaborate funeral was a favor she was doing herself, not McDivitt.

Afterward, she came to his noon Mass at St. Hilary's, her stated reason a desire to see the church where the final Mass for her grandfather would be said. But when they were seated at table in the rectory dining room, eating Marie Murkin's tuna salad, Beth said going to a weekday Mass reminded her of her school days.

"All that long ago?" Roger Dowling said with a smile.

"It seems long ago to me. There were Masses all over the campus and at different times of the day—early in the morning, at noon, late-evening Masses in some of the dorm chapels. It was hard not to go."

"It's not so easy after you start working."

"I wish I had kept it up. At school, I always prayed that my grandfather would be set free and proved innocent."

"Did you want your father arrested?"

"I hadn't made the connection then."

Roger Dowling was willing to wait for Beth to bring up the fake kidnapping from the school. When she did, she could not keep tears from her eyes.

"The whole idea was to really free him from the past. Oh sure, he was out of prison and could do what he wanted to, more or less, but my relatives were convinced he still had the money! They would not let him alone."

"What did he say when they brought up the money?"

"He refused to talk about it. Can you imagine anyone thinking he would have accepted prison if he didn't have to?"

"Did he ever express fear of anyone else?"

She looked at him abjectly. "I thought he was exaggerating! But it gave me the idea for the kidnapping. Grandpa would leave St. Hilary's early and come here; Laura would report a kidnapping and say she saw an Indiana plate. But Grandpa never showed up here. And then when you came with the news, I knew immediately. He really had been kidnapped!"

And Laura Zimmer, confusing reality with pretense, gave the number of the Indiana license plate.

Father Dowling put his hand on her arm. "Did he ever talk with you about the stolen money?"

She was silent for a moment. "I guess I can tell you. He was ashamed to tell me, but he seemed to feel he should. He began taking money because he intended to leave my grandmother. Just leave her. Go away. I try to remember her, but I can't, not really, so I don't know what his marriage was like, but that was his plan: embezzle enough money to desert his wife."

"Who then fell sick and died?"

"Grandpa thought he was being punished. By God. If he went to prison, it was to make up for the bad thing he had planned to do. And then to have the money stolen! But I think he was glad it had been."

"Is that what he said?"

She shook her head. "What he said was, 'Money isn't the root of all evil. It is the flower.'"

"What do you suppose he meant by that?"

"Money was never his motive. He wanted to be free of my grandmother. Well, he got his wish. And lost his freedom."

"Tell me about the kidnapping."

"Laura Zimmer had a crush on Grandpa. Maybe vice versa, but I don't know. He liked her well enough, and they talked, but he wasn't good with people. Maybe he had been once and lost the knack. Anyway I knew I could count on her, and he agreed."

"So he was in on it?"

"Father, it was as much his idea as mine."

"To get away from his relatives?"

"To get away from the past."

Which would have meant the past in prison too. Had the old man wanted to flee his greedy relatives or the greater menace of former fellow prisoners who would kill him for the money they thought he had? In the end they had done just that. The feared kidnapping prompted plans for a fake kidnapping, but then a real one had taken place.

"Where did your grandfather intend to go?"

"Arizona."

"Would his parole have permitted that?"

"That was why he went along with the kidnapping."

Phil Keegan too took a different view of it in the light of what had happened to Raymond Phillips.

"It was a damned foolish thing to do, Roger, but I suppose the girl realizes that now without being told. But did she really think that he went along with it only in order to dodge his sons?"

"Apparently."

"Well, now she knows why the old man agreed."

"She knew about the relatives. But how could she know about Phillips's fellow alumni from Joliet? For that matter, why was he himself suddenly concerned?"

They were seated in the rectory study, the hour was late, and Phil drained his glass of beer before answering. "Dwayne did call Phillips, Roger. He admitted that to Cy Horvath. One morning when he sobered up, he remembered sounding off to the wrong people about the old guy he had shared the cell with who had gone home to all that money. He had the good sense to warn Phillips."

"No wonder he wanted to disappear."

"And I tell you in confidence, Roger. Think of the spot Martin would be in if it became known what he told us."

"His friends seem willing to act on guesses. Maybe *he* should go to Arizona."

"Roger, all I could do is give him my word I would keep him out of it. We don't need him anyway. We have the ones who did it."

The priest shook his head sadly. "What did killing Phillips gain them?"

"Nothing. They killed him because kidnapping had gained them nothing. And left him where they did as a grisly thank you to Dwayne." Keegan looked at his watch and frowned. He was waiting to be told he had time for another beer before heading home. Roger Dowling told him.

When Phil came back from the kitchen, the local news had progressed to sports, and Roger Dowling turned up the sound. Phil's third beer and the sad tale of the Blackhawks and Bulls signalled the end of the evening, but long after Phil had left, Roger Dowling sat on in his study, puffing meditatively on his pipe. Before he went to bed, he had made up his mind. The next day he would go see Dwayne Martin.

The ex-convict was not happy to see him, although the Roman collar helped a little. But the fact that Father Dowling wanted to talk of Raymond Phillips made him very uncomfortable. They sat in a shack-like office that was heated to a turn by a kerosene space heater. The wall calendar devoted three times as much space to a nude woman as to the days of the month.

"Mr. Phillips had been coming to the St. Hilary parish center. We have a lot of old people."

"He told me about it."

"I understand you called him."

Martin sat forward, gripping the arms of the old wooden desk chair, whose spring squawked at the sudden motion. They were alone in the shack, but Martin spoke in a whisper.

"He came here. To see me."

"Phillips?"

"Yes."

"You were cell mates in Joliet, weren't you?"

"I liked him. And I'll tell you this, Father. He was a good Catholic. You should know that. Said his prayers morning and night, went to Mass every Sunday."

"I'm glad to hear that."

"In shop he made a statue of his favorite saint. Saint Anthony. Turned it on the lathe and then carved the rest. He had to do that in shop. He hollowed it out, and they didn't like that; they thought he might conceal something in it, but what could they do? He kept it in the cell. Ray liked shop. Funny thing, a bookkeeper like that, but he liked working with his hands. He even took up soldering. That's one reason he came here."

"Soldering?"

"The old-fashioned way. Melt lead in a pot and form pipe joints with it. No one does it that way anymore, not with copper pipe. Plastic pipe—who needs lead joints?"

"You two talked about soldering?"

"He wanted to know where he could get a kettle and heater. I got him one. He said maybe he would make lead soldiers. He was joking."

From the window of the shack, Roger Dowling had a vision of acres of departed automobiles, exposed to the weather, waiting to donate their parts, perhaps eventually to be melted down and used again.

"I wondered what happened to old cars."

"That's a fortune out there," Martin said. "It looks like junk, but it represents real money. I wish it belonged to me."

SEVEN

AFTER THE FUNERAL MASS and burial of Raymond Phillips, Beth put on a luncheon in her apartment in Oak Park, and it was there Father Dowling met her father. Maurice and Steve and their families were there too, but the uncles were as unprepossessing as their father had been, whereas Austin Phillips had panache. Beth had gotten her irrepressibility from him, clearly, but she had not inherited his dramatic looks. He looked Spanish, perhaps the result of his sojourn in Pamplona.

"Why Pamplona?" Father Dowling asked him.

He looked up from the diminutive sandwich he held. "Ever read *The Sun Also Rises?*"

"Hemingway? Years ago."

"I have read it at least once a year since I was seventeen. Much of the action of the novel takes place in Pamplona. There is a huge statue of Hemingway near the bullring."

"What do you do there?"

He had taken a bite of the sandwich and chewed thoughtfully before answering. "I am writing a novel."

"Ah. I thought you were in computers."

"So I was. I've sailed on many a sinking ship, Father Dowling."

"But some stayed afloat longer than others?"

"How do you mean?"

"The encyclopedias on computer disk scheme."

The man's face lit up at the memory. "Now, there was a great idea. Yes, before squalls hit, it did indeed have quite a little voyage."

"Thanks to your father?"

"That's right." He smiled. "One of the few debts I ever paid."

"Your father lent you money and you paid him back?"

"Not quite. He stood surety at his bank for a loan I got. Forty thousand for six months. And I paid it off in time!" He frowned. "I should have squirreled some away like my father."

So much for Beth's suspicions of her father, if the story was true. "Tell me about your novel."

"It's based on what happened to my father."

"What is the plot?"

"Surely you know the story."

"I have heard several versions."

Austin Phillips was delighted. "That's my plot. A certain set of events, half a dozen plausible explanations. Different characters accept different explanations because of what they are."

"It sounds fascinating."

He frowned. "It isn't easy to write."

"What version do you personally accept?"

He hesitated, then moved closer. "I can trust a priest. Father, my idea is that the money is still in the house."

"Hidden?"

"Hidden. The house was sold, and the proceeds went to the bank. It is my ambition to buy the house and subject it to a thorough search."

"Perhaps people who have lived there since have found it."

"Good! Of course I've thought of that. And I made certain they had not. I hired a private investigator."

"Did you trust him?"

"Oh, I gave him a wild explanation for wanting the information he provided me. And of course I did not use my own name."

"If the money is still there, that means your father went to prison rather than turn it over. Wouldn't he have retrieved it once he got out?"

"He was dying, Father. Leukemia. He would not have lived long in any case."

"So you think he just forgot about the money?"

"No. But I think he tried. When you say money, Father, what do you think of?"

"Bills?" He meant it as a joke.

"Right! Notes, paper. But what if he invested in silver or gold?"

"Who lives in your father's old house now?"

"A retired school teacher. Beth knows her."

"What is her name?"

"Laura Zimmer."

Roger Dowling let it go. Everything about Phillips seemed to move in circles. He went on to say a few words to the Indiana relatives. Unlike Austin, the other children of Raymond Phillips said nothing of the twice-stolen money, nor did they seem to have any curiosity about it. Maurice just shrugged, and Steve, who hated banks, said he doubted any money had ever been stolen. "At least by my father."

"Didn't he say it had been stolen from him in turn?"

"My mother's death changed him, Father. Sometimes I think he made the whole thing up. To punish himself." A little smile came and went. "When you have a wife, you don't have to punish yourself."

"It's so good to have everyone together again," Beth said. "Grandpa would have liked that."

He refused the stipend she handed him. "Not at all. I feel I owe it to him. And I shall continue to remember him in my prayers."

Her eyes filled with tears. "Do you know what I keep thinking? Now he's safe."

"You're right, you know."

"Grandpa kept telling me to practice my religion. In a nice way. He wasn't a nag. 'Always say your prayers,' that was his advice. And pray to St. Anthony."

"Especially when you lose something."

"Why is that?"

"St. Anthony is the one you pray to when you've lost something."

"And he helps you find it?"

"Try it."

"You sound like Grandpa."

LUNCH HAD BEEN SERVED in the parish center to the old people who had attended the funeral of Raymond Phillips. Joe Plaisance was reminiscing about the deceased when Father Dowling arrived from Oak Park. He stopped inside the auditorium. Laura Zimmer, in her wheelchair, made a disgusted noise.

"Listen to that man, Father. He wouldn't give Raymond the time of day when he was alive, and now they were best friends."

"You should have come to Oak Park."

She shook her head. "Beth understands. It was kind of her to ask me, though, and I appreciate it."

Roger Dowling drew a chair up beside Laura. "Did Beth know you bought her grandfather's house?"

"I didn't know it until Raymond told me. There was another owner before me. I didn't buy it from him. Or from the bank, as it would have been. I never told Beth. He asked me not to."

"Why did he mention it to you?"

"Nostalgia. He had raised his family in that house. I understood."

"Did he visit you there?"

"Twice. The first time, he just wandered through the house. I gave him the run of the place. Of course I avoid going upstairs now, because of my leg."

"And the second time?"

"He wanted to use the tool bench in the basement. He had learned a craft in prison that involved melting lead, and he brought his equipment along. It is still down there."

"Beth's father would like to buy the house back."

"He can have it immediately. It's too much house for me, Father. I want something all on one floor. Even after this leg heals, I don't want to be climbing stairs."

"I don't think he meant right away."

"I may not wait."

EIGHT

IT WAS A WEEK LATER that Edna Hospers brought the statue of St. Anthony of Padua to the rectory.

"He donated it to the parish, Father. I think you should have it." She held the statue as St. Anthony was holding the child Jesus.

"You don't want it in your office?"

She shook her head. "It saddens me to think of him. The poor old man."

He took the statue from her. It was surprisingly heavy, but since Edna did not comment on its weight, neither did he. She helped him make room for it on one of the book shelves.

When Phil Keegan came by that night, Father Dowling had to direct his attention to his new possession. Phil squinted at the statue, then nodded. "He make it?"

"In prison."

"He wasn't much of an artist."

"I think of it as a primitive."

Marie Murkin did not want to give her opinion of it, but when pressed she said she thought it was a dirty trick to play on St. Anthony. "That thing looks like some kind of heathen idol."

"You don't think it resembles St. Anthony?"

She was about to answer, but then she saw the trap and huffed from the study. That one statue did not look like another was hardly marks against it. Of course this one did not look much like a man either. Roger Dowling began to wonder about Edna's true motive in wanting it out of her office.

When Laura Zimmer's leg mended, she invited him for tea, and he went. "To get away from all the cocoa," he explained to Marie, who pretended not to hear.

"I don't see a For Sale sign out front," he said to Laura.

"Now that I'm not a cripple, I find I don't really want to leave this house."

"That will disappoint Austin Phillips."

"I never heard from him. If I had, I would have offered him the equipment Raymond left in the basement."

"Could I see it?"

"Just so you don't expect me to go down there."

The house was old, and pipes and ducts clung to the low ceiling of the basement. An oil burner had been added to what once must have been a coal furnace. The workbench was an ell-shaped surface in a corner of the basement. Tools were hung neatly above it as well as a row of bottles containing nails and screws and nuts and bolts. The little heater with the small kettle on it stood on the floor beside the workbench. Father Dowling picked up the kettle, tested its heft. A ladle with a curved arm was in the kettle. The priest scraped a yellowish substance that clung to the pouring lip of the ladle, then put it back in the kettle and the kettle back on the little stove.

Upstairs he asked Laura if Raymond Phillips had actually used the equipment here.

"Oh, yes."

"You're sure."

"Father, it filled the house with its smell, not an unpleasant smell, but distinctive."

"Did he bring lead with him?"

"Well he had a satchel."

When Roger Dowling thought of it during the next few days, he was reminded of the former prisoner in *A Tale of Two Cities* who turns to his shoe making in moments of crisis. Is that what molten lead had meant to Raymond Phillips?

It was exactly a week after Raymond Phillips's funeral that the pieces came together in Roger Dowling's mind. The occasion was a news broadcast featuring the falling dollar and the rising price of gold. He waited until Phil had left and, before he took the statue down from the shelf, closed his eyes and said a prayer to St. Anthony of Padua. He didn't ask for anything. "Think of it as a kind of salute," he told the saint.

He put the statue flat on the desk so that he could see the bottom. The old man's former cell mate, Dwayne Martin, had said the guards had not liked the fact that Phillips hollowed out the statue. It was no longer hollow. The question was, with what had it been filled? The statue was heavy as lead, and the metal that showed in the circular hole underneath the foot of the statue was dark. Leaden in color. The priest picked up a letter opener and began to dig into the lead.

The yellow began to show through after he had dug through an eighth of an inch of lead. Father Dowling tipped the statue toward the light. There seemed to be no doubt. It was gold. He sat there for a time, imagining the old man melting it down in that kettle and ladling it into this hollow statue, a memento of his prison years. What did that say of those long-ago events, the embezzlement, the reported theft, and all those years in prison?

Roger Dowling pressed the lead he had scraped away back where it had come from until nothing but lead was visible, then put the statue back on the shelf. When he looked at it now, he said another prayer to St. Anthony. What was he supposed to do?

He thought of giving it to Beth, or to her father, or to all the Phillipses to divide among themselves. But that is something Raymond Phillips could have done if he had wanted to. Instead he had given the money to the parish.

But he had not said it must be kept. Presumably, it could be used as the parish saw fit. Father Dowling decided to consider the gold a donation to the parish center. He looked at the statue Raymond Phillips had made. It was only his imagination of course, but St. Anthony seemed to be smiling in agreement.

The Dead Weight Lifter

A FATHER DOWLING
MYSTERY NOVELLA

THE OLD MAN was found lying on the steps of the school when Mrs. Hospers arrived to open up. One or two senior parishioners huddled some distance from the door, in a little patch of sunlight, keeping warm. Perhaps they thought their distance was a way of showing respect, on the assumption that it was a vagrant who had spent the night there and must soon wake and slink away ashamed. That the man was dead occurred to no one, so it fell to Mrs. Hospers to make the discovery.

Her scream, the way she scrambled back down the stairs, brought the others rushing to her side.

"Someone go for Father Dowling," she said, over her first shock, mindful that these elderly people were more or less her wards. But death was more fascinating than her wishes. Jaws slack, a wondering look in their eyes, they stared down at the man. How long before they themselves would go?

In the end, Edna Hospers went for the pastor herself.

"Are you sure he's dead?" Roger Dowling asked, rising from the table. In the kitchen door Marie

Murkin, the housekeeper, twisted her hands in her apron.

"I think so."

"I'll bring the oils anyway."

"I'll call the paramedics," Marie said.

Edna ran back to the school, where a large crowd had gathered. Austin Beatty, one of the old people, was kneeling beside the body, and several others, thinking he was praying, lowered themselves arthritically to their knees. But Austin rose in a minute and turned away.

"He's dead," he said to Mrs. Hospers.

"Father Dowling is coming. Mrs. Murkin called an ambulance."

"He's still dead," Austin said and shambled back into the sunlight.

It was a nerve-wracking way to start a day—and a week, Edna reflected, when Father Dowling had given the last rites and the paramedics had decided there was nothing they could do.

There was no identification on the body.

Father Dowling did not accept Edna's offer to sit when he came by her office.

"Edna, last month there was a man who spent the night curled against the wall of the boiler room. Now this. We can't have it. We're going to have to provide sleeping quarters for poor devils like that."

"Two is not a trend, Father."

"But how many would there be if we provided shelter?"

"We're not on the beaten path for that sort of thing, Father. The man a month ago was lost. Who knows why this man chose to come to St. Hilary's and die?"

"I wonder who he was?"

Since he knew that question would pester him until he had an answer to it, Roger Dowling checked with the hospital to see if any identification had turned up there. The body had already been sent on to the morgue. Such efficiency suddenly seemed ghoulish, though the reaction was unfair. The morgue was awaiting instructions, but an autopsy would be performed. Roger Dowling put in a call to Phil Keegan, and his old friend the Fox River captain of detectives was not particularly moved by the story.

"Was there any evidence of foul play, Roger?"

"He looked as if he died in his sleep. But of course I don't know."

"Who was he?"

"That's the eerie thing. There was no identification on the body. It doesn't seem right that a person should leave this life so anonymously."

"It happens all the time."

"Not on the steps of St. Hilary's school it doesn't."

"You sure he isn't someone who's been coming there?"

Because of the changes wrought in the parish by several interstates and the general flow to the more pleasant suburbs, St. Hilary's parish in Fox River, Illinois, no longer had a need for its parish school. An attractive building in good repair, it seemed a shame simply to shut it up. So Roger Dowling had turned it into a center where the elderly could spend the day, under the general tutelage of Edna Hospers and various volunteers, but not overly organized. If they wanted to spend the day just talking, that was all right.

"He would have been recognized, Phil."

"I suppose they'd have sent the body on to the morgue by now."

"They have. Would you look into it, Phil?"

Phil said he would, but he could not keep from his voice the feeling that Roger Dowling was overreacting.

It would have been presumptuous to have a religious ceremony for the stranger, but that did not prevent Father Dowling from saying a prayer for the repose of the unknown's soul. There was some consolation in realizing that he was not unknown to God.

Marie tapped on the door, leaned into the study and whispered, "One of the old fellows wants to talk with you."

How relative age is. The presence of those elderly men and women had done a world of good for Marie

Murkin. Suddenly in her fifties she was, relatively speaking, a spring chicken.

"Who is it?"

"Austin Beatty," a man behind Marie said, and she turned to give him a look. No one got to the pastor except through Marie Murkin if she could help it.

"Come in, Austin."

Middle height, a bit overweight, iron grey hair still thick and wavy, he tipped his head and found the lens he wanted. Marie's tone had suggested that his visitor would be someone upset by the events of the morning, but Austin Beatty did not look like a man easily upset.

"That man found dead this morning?"

Father Dowling nodded. "I still haven't found out who he is."

"His name's Potter. Fielding Potter. He lives right here in Fox River."

"Sit down, Austin. Do you drink coffee?"

"Is it decaf?"

"That's against my religion, I'm afraid."

"Mine too. Can't stand it. You got the real thing, I'll have a cup."

Roger Dowling filled a mug from the Mr. Coffee that was always going in his study. "Now then, you say his name is Fielding Potter."

"That's right." Austin sipped the coffee, approved, and sipped some more. "Don't know what he was doing on those steps. He's not a Catholic. More important, he is a wealthy man."

"How come you recognized him?"

"I worked for him for thirty years."

Roger Dowling got out the phone book and looked up Potter. There were two listings in Fox River, Fielding and Regis.

"Regis is the nephew."

"I suppose I should call him. Or is there someone at his house?"

"There is unless his daughter, Emily, finally got married and moved away, but I haven't heard of it."

The priest dialed the number of Fielding Potter and listened as the phone rang and rang. He was just about to hang up when a sepulchral feminine voice said hello.

"Is this the home of Fielding Potter?"

A long pause. "Yes."

"Is he there?"

"If you are selling something, we are not interested. Good-bye."

"Wait! This is Father Roger Dowling, pastor of St. Hilary's church."

The phone had not been hung up. After a very long pause, the woman said, "I beg your pardon."

"Is your father there?"

"Why do you ask?"

Father Dowling fought his impatience. "Because an elderly man was found dead on the steps of the parish school this morning, and someone thinks it is your father."

A shorter pause. "What is the address?"

"He's no longer here. We called an ambulance, but it was too late. He is now at the morgue. I am very sorry to be telling you these terrible things."

"You say someone thought he was my father." There was no change in her voice, but then it had been mournful from the beginning.

"There was no identification on the body."

"Ah. It cannot be my father."

"Why?"

"My father is in Florida."

"If I'm mistaken, I am very sorry...." But across the desk, Austin Beatty shook his head from side to side.

"It's Potter," he said.

"Miss Potter, the man who thinks it is your father tells me he has no doubt it is."

"What should I do?"

"Someone should go to the morgue and identify the body. That is not a pleasant task."

"I will do it at once."

"If you would like someone to go with you..."

A pause. "If you have a car, that would make it less inconvenient."

"I'll come by for you in half an hour."

"Could we say an hour?"

"Of course."

When Father Dowling hung up, Austin Beatty expressed surprise that Emily Potter herself would go. "She almost never leaves the house. Likes being by herself. What kind of a wreck do you call a person like that?"

"A recluse?"

"That's it."

"Did you ever see her?"

"Once. I took something to the house for Mr. Potter, and when she realized I wasn't leaving until the door was answered, she came down. What I saw was one arm and the tip of her nose."

"Tell me about Fielding Potter."

From Austin Beatty's remarks and later inquiry, the picture of Fielding Potter that emerged was this. He had broken with his family in Mobile when he was a young man and come north to make his fortune. So far as formal education went, he had been to grade school and three years of high school; but in the college of experience, he had an advanced degree. He found work with a printer, went on to newspaper work, ending in classified ads when, at twenty-nine, he left to begin the first of the shoppers guides that would make his fortune.

The paper was distributed free at every door in town, and that guaranteed circulation enabled Potter to attract advertising revenue from the most modest to the full-page variety. His rates were better than the newspapers, and his paper was read chiefly for two reasons. Personal ads were run gratis and Potter himself, under the pen name Jeff Davis, wrote a gossip column that was ninety percent fiction but no less avidly read for that. Potter was the first to admit it was the personals that explained why his paper was really read. These notices were not as candid as personals have subsequently become, but when they began to appear, they were daring enough for the time. Potter was sued early and often by irate husbands claiming his paper had aided in alienating the affection of their wives. Some matron wistfully responding to a plea for friendship in a personal ran off with the grocery money and the man. The publicity far outweighed the nuisance, and it was said that Potter came to hope for litigation.

From Fox River he had branched out to other communities, and in every case the Jeff Davis column and the free personals led to success. At the peak of his career, Fielding Potter owned a chain of such shopping guides that blanketed the towns that were to become the western suburbs of Chicago.

Fielding Potter was eighty-two when he retired. He kept an office in the building he put up near a cloverleaf of interstates, a squat block of a building, all copper-colored glass. He continued to go to his office at least once a week, keeping the reins of power as he had kept his business a family corporation with his nephew Regis as heir apparent.

THE POTTER PROPERTY was surrounded by a wrought-iron fence marked at intervals of twenty feet by brick columns of striking and elaborate design. The gate was closed, but when Roger Dowling turned in, a voice seemed to speak from the heavens.

"Is that Reverend Dowling?"

"Yes, it is."

The gate swung slowly open and the voice spoke again. "Please drive in."

It would have been a good walk to the house. The grounds were striking because of the Spanish moss hanging from some of the trees, and the terraced formal garden that seemed embraced by the wings of the mansion. Although it was built of brick, there was a soupçon of the South in its high-columned porch. As he drew to a stop beneath the porte cochere, a woman emerged from the house.

She wore a lavender turban, her face was powdered chalk white, her sunglasses were opaque and, although it was April, she had on a fur coat that fell to her ankles. Father Dowling leaned over to open the door, and she extended a gloved hand.

"I am Emily Potter."

"Roger Dowling."

She slid in beside him, wrapping her coat about her, and immediately the car was filled with her perfume.

When Roger Dowling was in the seminary, the spiritual director had often urged on them the need for prudence in their deportment with women. One must avoid even the breath of scandal, he would say, one hand clamped to his cheek, its little finger fluttering before his puckered lips as if he were eliciting music from it. They had all thought old Father Brady excessive in his sense of propriety. Now for the first time, Roger Dowling wished he had followed Brady's advice and put Emily Potter in the back seat.

"I still do not think the man you spoke of is my father."

"Did you try reaching him in Florida?"

"He might not have heard the phone. His hearing is bad. It is an inherited defect." She pulled back her turban to display a hearing aid. "Both sides," she added. "My father doesn't always wear his. I understand. The world of silence is preferable. You are a Catholic priest?"

"Yes."

"We are not Catholics."

"What are you?"

He could feel her eyes or at least her dark glasses on him. "Just non-Catholics, I guess."

"If your father had a church . . ."

"He avoided them. They did not avoid him, of course. He was besieged by requests for money."

Father Dowling smiled. "Was he generous?"

"He is a stingy and avaricious man. He made a fortune unaided. He believes anyone else can do the same."

The attendant at the morgue could not disguise her reaction to Emily Potter. She led them to a room, pointed out the TV set, and left.

"I never watch television," Emily said.

But when the face of the man who had been found on the steps of St. Hilary's school came on the screen, she stood and went closer to the screen. She took off her glasses, but her back was to him, so Roger Dowling did not see her eyes. She began to nod slowly. She put on her glasses.

"That is my father," she said.

Then she sank slowly to the floor, and for the second time that morning, Roger Dowling was bending over the body of a member of the Potter family.

WHEN PHIL KEEGAN called to say they had a make on the body at the morgue, Roger Dowling did not mention that he had been there when the identification was made. But he did mention Austin Beatty.

"Worked for him thirty years? What does that mean, he peddled one of the papers?"

"I didn't ask. Are you coming by tonight?"

"Aren't the Cubs on?"

"I believe they are."

"It's possible that Fielding Potter said he wouldn't be found dead in a Catholic church," Phil mused that evening. "It was the only way he got close to one anyhow."

"What do you know of the family?"

"About as much as I know of the Rockefellers. What I read in the paper. Roger, they're rich. Wealthy. Hundreds of millions."

"I met Emily."

Phil squinted at Roger during the recital of the visit to the morgue.

"Well, aren't you the sly one. You might have told me."

"I wanted you to drop by."

"The Cubs are excuse enough for that."

The National League team played a lackluster game that did not interfere with their conversation. Phil had a surprise of his own.

"It looks as if someone might have helped Fielding Potter into the next world."

"Killed him?"

"Smothered him, the coroner thinks. It could have been a mugger, I suppose, who then removed all identification from the body."

"A mugger at St. Hilary's?"

"It's as likely as having Potter showing up dead on your steps one morning."

"You don't believe that."

"No. There's nothing that proves he died where he was found."

"So you're treating it as homicide?"

"But discreetly. I don't want a lot of journalists breathing down my neck."

That proved to be an unanswered prayer. Even as they spoke, Merlin of the *Fox River Tribune* telephoned, wondering if Father Dowling had any idea where he could reach Captain Keegan. Roger covered the phone and told Phil who it was. A moral struggle went on across Phil's broad face, and then he reached for the phone.

"Keegan." He closed his eyes and drummed his fingers on the desk. "That's right. He was found collapsed this morning. Paramedics were called but it was too late." He opened his eyes, then closed them again. "A public place. As on the street. Close to St. Hilary's church. Mrs. Hospers found him. What? Sure." He thrust the phone at Roger.

"I guess I should have talked with you in the first place, Father."

Roger Dowling told Merlin the truth, though not all of it. He omitted any mention of the fact that there was no identification on the body or that his daughter thought he was in Florida. But he told Phil after he had finished talking with Merlin.

"He has another estate in Sarasota. Tried starting a paper down there, but it didn't fly."

"Phil, he wasn't mugged. Who killed him?"

"I don't know. I put Cy Horvath and Agnes Lamb on it. They were going to talk with the nephew tonight."

"Regis?"

"Don't tell me you took him for a ride today too? How did you manage to get Emily home?"

"Indirectly. I insisted she should be checked at emergency. Once she was in good hands, I left her there."

"Not very gallant of you."

"Did you ever know Father Brady?"

"At Quigley?"

"No, this was later, at Mundelein."

"Quigley was as late as I got. Why?"

"It's a long story. I wonder what Agnes and Cy will learn from Regis Potter."

IT WAS AFTER Phil had left, after midnight actually, that Emily Potter called. "Regis will be furious, but I want you to conduct a service for my father. I have never known a Catholic priest, and I doubt that he did. But he had no other clerical friends either." She paused. "He did not have a gift for friends. But it's not just because there's no one else. You befriended him in death. And I would like prayers said for him. I myself do not believe in God."

"Did your father?"

"We never discussed it. But if there is a God, what difference will it make whether he believed in him? He would need prayers all the more."

So it was that on Wednesday morning Roger Dowling arrived at the Chadwick mortuary at ten in the morning and was ushered by Chadwick junior to the parlor, where the ashes of Fielding Potter were enshrined in a modest urn, burnished bronze, surrounded by flowers.

"We haven't seen much of you, Father," Chadwick purred as they walked.

"Healthy parishioners," Roger said.

"I had wondered if I might come talk to the retired people who spend their days with you."

"You'd have to ask Mrs. Hospers."

Most St. Hilary funerals were carried out by McDivitt. Chadwick was twice as expensive, and both father and son had a manner that suggested that the social differences of this world carry over into the next, so why not buy the best? Roger quelled the desire to ask young Chadwick if he had visited the King Tut exhibit when it was in Chicago.

There were seven people in the room, and one turned out to be a Chadwick employee. Of the others, Roger knew only Emily. She wore a black velvet turban today but otherwise looked as she had on Monday. Her gloved hand detained his for a moment. "How good of you to come."

She introduced him to two men, Folwell and Earl, who were high in the Potter hierarchy, and their wives, all four looking a bit embarrassed to have to acknowledge mortality, and then, with seeming reluctance, to her cousin Regis. She immediately drifted away.

"We don't get along," Regis said with a smile. He seemed to have more than the usual number of teeth. "Thanks for what you did for my uncle, Father. And thanks for coming here. Fielding Potter was an old heathen, but he knew the Bible like the back of his hand. I think he would appreciate the humor of a Catholic priest praying over his ashes. No offense."

He put a hand on Father Dowling's arm and exposed several more teeth. Roger Dowling knew a good deal about Regis Potter because of the efforts of Horvath and Lamb, passed on to him over the phone by Phil.

Regis had majored in drama at Northwestern and had appeared in several movies as well as on television, and at sixty still had the manner of a man who was sure a camera was focused on him from somewhere. Twenty years ago, recognizing that his acting was at best competent, he petitioned his uncle for a job and was taken on. Regis had had the notion he would be a great help to his uncle, being fresh from the wider world, but he soon learned that in his chosen field no one knew more than Fielding Potter. Regis, come to patronize, stayed to praise. His admiration for his uncle was sincere, but there were those, and Emily was among them, who considered his constant praise of Fielding Potter to be purposed. More surprising, perhaps, was the obvious pleasure the old man took from hearing someone tell him what a truly remarkable man he was. Regis rose like cream in the company and, if his uncle had ever retired, he would have been undisputed boss long ago. As it was, any decision of his was subject to Fielding's veto, and the old man used it with the gusto of a lame-duck president vetoing congress.

And so, in Chadwick's mortuary, when Regis's smile was conferring importance on him, Roger tried unsuccessfully to pierce the facade. Had this man, out of patience at last, smothered his uncle and then put the body in a wholly unpredictable place to divert attention from himself?

"Why remove all identification then?" Phil had asked when he put the question to him.

"Just to mystify."

"But why? The old man is found dead. Not so far from his home that he might not have walked."

"At eighty-two?"

"He could do it. Roger, this guy ran two miles every morning. He had his own masseur and physical trainer, lives right at the house. So let him go for a walk and keel over."

Roger had no reply to that, and getting a good look at Regis brought him no closer to one.

He read from the Book of Wisdom. He read from Acts the account of Christ's resurrection. He read a few verses of Paul. And then, why not, this wasn't a liturgy, he read some Tennyson. And finally he asked God to have mercy on the soul of Fielding Potter and welcome him into eternal happiness.

When he turned, tears were leaking from under Emily's glasses, making little arroyos down her powdered cheeks. Again she gripped his hand.

"I particularly liked the Tennyson," she said in her sepulchral voice. Regis joined them and she took back her hand.

"And now for the reading of the will?" He leered at Emily and she spun away. Regis winked at Father Dowling. "Not that there will be any surprises."

"Who was his lawyer?"

"Amos Cadbury."

"Ah."

"Do you know him?"

"As a matter of fact I do."

An electric light gleamed metaphorically over Regis's head. He could easily have acted in silent movies.

"Why don't you come to the house then? The rest of us are going. There'll be a brunch."

"And the reading of the will?"

The smile went, although his lips had trouble eclipsing his teeth. He was looking over Roger Dowling's shoulder at the urn.

"I'm going to miss Uncle Fielding. We knew he would go sometime, and sooner rather than later, but still it's sad."

"There wasn't anything wrong with him, was there?"

"With Fielding? You and I should be in such good health. He was old, of course, and people do not live forever. Though he had said he was determined to see one hundred. The way he worked out with Bruno, his trainer, I'm surprised he didn't."

"What was the cause of death?"

An expression of total surprise. "I never asked. I assume it was old age."

"Regis invited me to the house," he said to Emily as they were leaving.

"Why?" she asked and then searched for his hand, but he gripped his books. "I mean why did *he* ask. But you must come."

He was more repelled than attracted. The prospect of watching heirs learn that they were going to be even wealthier than they had been was not high on his list of things to do. But the image of that elderly man lying dead on the steps of St. Hilary's school, cast aside like rubbish, deprived of his identity, moved him. He would find it difficult to rest until he knew what had happened and, if it had been made to happen, by whom. Phil Keegan would see this as a crime and want justice to be done, but Roger Dowling had another viewpoint. If murder had been committed, that is, a sin, then there must be a sinner, and what sinners need is mercy. In God, justice and mercy may be one, but here below they tend to clash, which is why he and Phil sometimes had misunderstandings.

EMILY, thank God, was taken by the Folwells, so it was alone that Roger Dowling once more drove up the long drive to the Potter mansion. And he could not help but think how oddly lives end. After more than eighty years, a moment came that was the last for Potter, and yet things went on; his relatives converged on his house to learn what his will for them was, a last word from beyond the grave.

Folwell and Earl and their wives fell upon the food as if they had just discovered their reason for being. After an unusual morning, finally something familiar. There was a champagne cocktail, scrambled eggs, sausages, bacon, ham, French toast and ordinary toast, and coffee, an extremely good coffee. Father Dowling took some French toast and coffee and followed the Folwells and the Earls toward the living room, but on the way he encountered Cadbury.

To say that Amos Cadbury, Fox River's premier lawyer, was surprised to see him there was an understatement, but his reaction was nothing compared with that he gave Regis's account of the service at the mortuary. He couldn't wait to get Father Dowling aside, steering him into the kitchen, where a cook and a burly man who seemed about to burst from his shirt stopped talking when they entered. Cadbury waved at them, urging them to go on doing whatever they were doing.

"Don't tell me Fielding Potter is a convert of yours."

"Only posthumously."

Cadbury thought about that and decided it didn't make sense. "I don't understand."

"His body was found on the steps of St. Hilary's school."

"Really. The newspaper was not so precise. I gathered he had just been felled while out walking."

"The family thought he was in Florida."

"Regis?"

"No. Emily."

Cadbury permitted his eyes to flicker heavenward. "Fielding was not in the habit of keeping Emily well informed on his doings."

"You must tell me about Emily sometime."

"Oh, what a story. Tragic love, thwarted elopement, decades spent writing unreadable verse."

"But surely she would have known whether her father was home or not?"

"That seems a reasonable assumption. But not with Emily."

Regis found them. "Conspiring with the lawyer? Amos, this man will have his parish benefit from events no matter what. I'm kidding." The hand on the arm. "We are deeply indebted to Father Dowling."

"We are old friends," Amos said. "When shall we begin?"

"What was it Uncle Fielding used to say? 'Possums ain't caught till they's caught.' I'm ready."

Cadbury set up shop at one end of the dining-room table, telling the Folwells and Earls to please continue eating, this wouldn't take long at all.

"There have been some recent changes," he said, moving his glasses to his forehead, then lowering them again. "But I doubt that anyone will be severely disappointed." A little bow of a smile, and then he began to read. Roger Dowling did not follow the details. It was written in the jargon devised to make such documents crystal clear to anyone who had lost his sense of ordinary language.

Intelligible to brother lawyers, that is. Regis was named president of the family corporation; Folwell and Earl were continued on the board, thanked for loyal service over the years, and given equal and ample amounts. Their spouses stopped chewing for a moment, then resumed with vigor. Emily got the house they were in; Regis one in Sarasota. After the accounting, eighty percent of the net worth was to be divided between them: forty-five percent to Emily; thirty-five to Regis. Neither her powdered face nor his radiant smile altered as this was read. But the fifteen percent of net left to Bruno Armshlager, Fielding's physical-exercise man and masseur, caused a stir. Roger Dowling had noticed Cadbury whisper to Bruno before they left the kitchen, and he had been standing unobtrusively in the little hallway since Cadbury began.

"Did you say fifteen percent, old sport?" Regis asked. He had had a bit part in an early and live TV presentation of *The Great Gatsby,* and the effect had been lasting.

"That's right."

"With all due respect for my uncle's soundness of mind, isn't that a little strange?"

"We discussed it before the change was made," Cadbury said. "He was adamant. And his mind was sound as a dollar."

"He thought that exercise would make him live till a hundred."

Bruno's face looked like a shadowgraph made with a fist. If he resented this discussion, there was no way to tell from his expression.

"Wasn't it the exercise that killed him?" Mrs. Folwell said and then looked as though she were going to clamp a hand over her mouth.

Cadbury took advantage of her embarrassment to finish reading. People Roger Dowling assumed were staff and clerical help were provided for, though in a much much more modest way than Bruno.

As Cadbury was scooping up his papers, Roger Dowling asked him, sotto voce, what fifteen percent of the net worth came to.

Cadbury wobbled his hand. "At the least, twenty million; at the most nearly thirty."

He had not spoken in a whisper. Mouths fell open all around the table.

"That's absurd," Regis said, and he wasn't smiling at all.

"There are other absurdities in the will," Emily informed the ceiling.

Cadbury said, "There are legal steps you could take. I do not recommend them. Indeed, I will defend this will to my dying breath."

They left together, and on the drive Roger Dowling asked, "What was your reaction when Fielding Potter left that much to Bruno?"

Amos did not hesitate. "I thought he was crazy."

"You said his mind was sound as a dollar."

"Yes." The little bow of a smile. "A confederate dollar. He wrote a column under the name Jeff Davis, you know."

"So I've heard."

Cadbury looked back at the house. "Everyone of the people there was treated better than he deserved. But I do not think they will let Bruno have his portion uncontested."

"Amos, have you spoken with the police about the way Mr. Potter died?"

"I noticed that Captain Keegan has been trying to reach me. I mean to return his call when I get back to my office."

"Fielding may have been killed, Amos."

"What?"

"Smothered. Smothered and then brought to St. Hilary's and left on the steps of the school with no identification on him."

"But why haven't I been told this?"

"Return Captain Keegan's call."

Again Cadbury looked back to the house, this time with an expression of wonderment on his face. He turned to his companion and nodded. ''I intend to. Goodbye, Father Dowling.''

He slid into the back seat of the gleaming black car with grey upholstery that had been waiting for him, and it began to move soundlessly away.

When Roger Dowling emerged from the gate of the Potter property in his nine-year-old Omega, he was glad to get away from the land of the rich.

He glanced at his watch. He would have to hurry to be on time for the Mass he said at noon.

DURING THE REST of that week, the investigation of the death of Fielding Potter went discreetly on, all but fading from the newspapers, although Merlin was said to have written thousands of words that did not find their way into print, until Regis Potter, true to Cadbury's prediction, began a court action to modify his uncle's will in the case of Bruno Armschlager.

''On what grounds?'' Roger Dowling asked Merlin, who had come to talk again about the precise manner of the discovery of the body of Fielding Potter.

''Fear. Suasion. Maybe he literally twisted his arm.''

''Cadbury will fight it.''

''Regis Potter has put the matter in Tuttle's hands.''

"Tuttle! Surely you're not serious."

Tuttle was a particularly vivid example of what happens when the ranks of lawyers swell. More tenacious than gifted, he survived in a highly competitive environment by using tactics that ran from the tasteless through the unethical and very nearly to the criminal. A slightly comic figure with a tweed Irish hat pulled low over his eyes regardless of season, Tuttle was an extraordinary choice for Regis to make.

"Maybe Cadbury recommended him." Merlin grinned. "I'm kidding. I think Regis figured that talents such as Tuttle's may be just what are needed to shake the patrician loftiness of Amos Cadbury. In any case, a plausible argument can be made."

"Because Bruno is strong?"

"I can see him carrying Potter through the deserted night streets and dumping him on the school steps." Merlin's eyes narrowed as this sentence, typical of his prose, rolled from his lips. Had the event taken on reality from being expressed?

The task of getting Potter to where he had been found was, Roger Dowling conceded, not negligible. He had the idea that Bruno would not fare well in the stories Merlin would write, given carte blanche at last by his editor because of Regis's suit.

"You neglected to mention earlier that there was no identification on the body." Merlin looked hurt. "I can see others conspiring to shield the wealthy and powerful, but not you.''

''Since I did not know who he was, shielding was hardly a possibility.''

''But we talked after you knew.''

''Merlin, I won't argue with you, but there are motives other than wanting to shield the rich to exercise restraint in such matters.''

Merlin looked skeptical. ''Why were you there at the reading of the will?''

''It took place after the memorial service at Chadwick's, and I was asked along. Curiosity overwhelmed me.''

''Memorial service?''

''The family asked me to say a few words.''

''For Fielding Potter!''

''Think of it as shielding the rich and powerful.''

''From the wrath of God?''

''We are all deserving of that, aren't we?''

He went with Merlin to the school, to shield Edna Hospers from the reporter, but she gave a crisp, accurate account, stuck with it, and Merlin decided to take it as such. Roger Dowling noticed that she named none of the old people who had been there, as he had not. Did Merlin imagine that they were not reliable witnesses? People had a way of condescending to the elderly, which, the priest thought, must be one of the greatest crosses of age. Certainly there was nothing wrong with Austin Beatty's mind.

"I understand you met the family, Father," Austin said, standing athwart the path to the rectory.

"What exactly did you do for Fielding Potter?"

"I made him rich." The solemn look was replaced by a broad smile. "He certainly didn't make me rich. I was in charge of circulation."

"I thought his papers are given away."

"Yes. But they have to get to the doorsteps. That may sound simple, but it isn't. Who will complain if he receives no copy of a paper to which he has not subscribed? It is a great temptation for carriers to simply dump their papers. My job consisted largely of policing the carriers."

"Were the carriers well paid?"

"They would have done better on welfare. Potter was not disposed to pay much for such unskilled labor, and he thought, rightly, that there was an infinite supply of people willing to do it. Of course that added to my problems. Once people took the job, they quickly resented the pay."

"You mean you actually went around checking on carriers?"

"Very seldom personally, though I did a bit of it myself. My man on the street was Bruno Armschlager."

"Well, well. He has come into his own, hasn't he?"

"Yes, and he deserves every penny. It's good to know that for once in his life old Potter showed some gratitude."

It was a change to hear someone who did not resent the silent masseur's good fortune. But of course Austin Beatty did not suffer from Bruno's gain.

"If he manages to get it," Roger Dowling said.

"Isn't that the way, Father? The nephew has more money now than he could spend, yet he resents Bruno's getting a little bit."

"I understand that little bit could run as much as thirty million dollars."

"Okay, but what did Regis ever do to deserve so much more? Except be related to Fielding."

"Regis was not an asset to the firm?"

"Oh, he was. I shouldn't exaggerate. But why can't he accept what his uncle wanted to do for Bruno if he can accept what he did for him?"

Because, Roger Dowling thought, when he was back in his study and had lit his pipe, because greed is abstract, almost spiritual. The avaricious person does not want *things* as such, he wants the sense of independence wealth gives or at least seems to give. The pursuit of it is finally a protest against the inevitability of death, and that is why it is not a materialistic but a profoundly spiritual flaw. It is the recognition that the wealth one has, however great, cannot stave off death that explains the constant pursuit of more.

It is also why everyone, rich and poor, is open to avarice.

These thoughts were interrupted by a phone call from Emily Potter, who wondered if Father Dowling could come to the house immediately.

"This is rather an emergency, Father. You mustn't think I am determined to pester you because you were once kind to me."

"An emergency?"

"It has to do with Regis's legal action. Bruno is with me."

Dowling said he would come, and so twenty minutes later he turned for the third time into the Fielding driveway, was invited by Emily's voice to enter, and proceeded to the house. The imposing figure of Bruno Armschlager awaited him on the steps.

"Miss Emily has gone to the gazebo. I'll take you there."

He turned and started across the lawn, and Roger Dowling fell in step with him, but it was not easy to hold to the pace set.

"I didn't get a chance to congratulate you on your good fortune when the will was read."

Bruno's profile was like a clinched fist. Did his frown deepen? For an answer, he shrugged.

"What will you do with all that money?"

"I don't want it!" He blurted this out as they came round the house with the gazebo straight ahead.

And that was the emergency Emily had called him to discuss. Bruno, offended by the reaction to the provision made for him in Fielding Potter's will, had decided to refuse to accept anything. He was content to let Emily speak for him.

"Of course he must do nothing of the kind. Regis cannot possibly break the will. Amos Cadbury assures me of that."

"I don't want the money," Bruno repeated as urgently as before.

Emily ignored him. "Admittedly a transition from the modest salary he has been receiving to the life of a millionaire poses problems. I have been trying to instruct him on that. I am a millionaire, for heaven's sake, or so I have always been told. Now it is a matter of public news. And what real difference does it make?" She patted her maroon turban, adjusted her dark glasses, and disturbed the chalky blankness of her face with a smile. "One of the options open to one with money is to live modestly."

"I don't need money to live the way I want," Bruno said.

Emily continued to address the priest. "And I have told him of the joys of philanthropy. He could endow..." She sought a likely object of Bruno's benevolence, and then she had it. "A gymnasium!" She turned to the reluctant millionaire. "What would you think of that, Bruno?"

"I don't want the money."

She shooed him away, telling Roger Dowling in amused tones that Bruno lifted enormous weights in order to relax.

"I wanted you to know this, Father. You and Amos Cadbury are friends. Amos, I am certain, requires no inducement to see that my father's will is carried out as written. Nonetheless, your moral support of his resolution may be appreciated."

"But what is to stop Bruno from refusing to take the money?"

"Oh, it will be his, no matter what. Making him keep it is another matter. But I assure you, the Fielding estate will not accept such a gift from Bruno Armschlager."

Emily wanted to speak of her soul, then, but when it became clear that this meant an account of the great love affair that had wounded her for life, Roger Dowling said he had to get back to the rectory.

"It is my job to be available."

"And only to your parishioners?"

"You must come see me at the rectory." It was a calculated gamble, but if she did come it would be almost worth it to see Marie Murkin's reaction to this incredible woman.

"I shall, Father. I shall. I am just now beginning to get intimations of the value of spiritual consolation."

PHIL KEEGAN CALLED three hours later to say that Cy Horvath had just arrested Bruno Armschlager.

"What on earth for?"

"The prosecutor's office is still working on the precise indictment. Failing to report a crime, for starters."

"What crime?"

"The murder of Fielding Potter."

"And Bruno was a witness?"

"At least. He must have known something. He was the one who put Potter's body where you found it."

"How did you learn that?"

"Potter's clothes have fibers from a flannel warm-up jacket of Bruno's. Which in turn has fibers from Potter's clothing. Suggesting that he carried the old man."

"Phil, even Tuttle could defend him against that. The two men worked out together daily."

"Roger, Potter was eighty-two years old."

"I know. But everyone insists he had become an exercise freak. He ran several miles every day."

"I would have to see that to believe it."

"Isn't that the way a jury would feel about Bruno's carrying the old man to the school steps? Why there, for heaven's sake?"

"I have been waiting for you to illumine me on that score."

Of course Roger Dowling had given the matter much thought. Why would anyone put the body of Fielding Potter on the steps of St. Hilary's school? An obvious answer was that it might have been anywhere, and it just happened to be the school. Which was the answer Roger gave to Phil Keegan's question. But, alone with his pipe, he was far from satisfied. It was as though there were something symbolic, something intended, in putting the old man there. But what possible connection was there between Fielding Potter and St. Hilary's school? If the old man had been a parishioner, if as a boy he had attended the school, if... And then he thought of Austin Beatty.

It was the only connection he knew between Potter and the school, tenuous as it was. He picked up the phone and rang Edna Hospers. No answer, but five minutes later he tried again and she answered.

"How often does Austin Beatty come here, Edna?"

"Oh, he's become one of the regulars. And he tells others about it. There must be ten others who come because of Austin's publicizing of what we're doing."

Other former employees of Fielding Potter? Not a question he could put to Edna.

"Is he around today?"

"I saw him ten minutes ago."

"Would it be too much trouble to ask him to come see me?"

"Will do."

But Austin did not come. Edna called back to say he had left for the day. "A friend of his is in some kind of trouble, and he has gone to see him."

"What kind of trouble?"

"I was told Austin went downtown to the jail."

Cadbury was furious. "I will defend the man myself, Father Dowling. This is all part of Regis's attempt to break his uncle's will, and I won't have it. My clients have a right to expect my steadfast loyalty, in death as in life, and I will not stand by while stunts like this are pulled."

"Regis Potter did not arrest Bruno; the police did."

"And how did they get hold of the supposed evidence?"

Roger Dowling remained silent. He knew that Agnes Lamb had slipped away to the gym while Cy Horvath interrogated Bruno and that the warm-up jacket had been spirited away at the time. After being examined it had been spirited back, the police returned with a court order, and soon after, Bruno had been arrested.

"I understand there is proof that Bruno carried the old man, Amos."

"Of course he had. He carried him every day. Fielding had become a fanatic. He had actually put before himself the goal of a five-mile run. He pushed himself incredibly, to the point of exhaustion. Father Dowling, I myself have seen Bruno help him up, support him and, yes, actually carry him. It is because of that devotion that Fielding was so generous to the man."

"If you can testify to that, there won't be much of a case."

"If I can't prevent it from going to trial, I won't be much of a lawyer. I promise you I will have him out of jail within the hour."

PHIL KEEGAN CAME TO the noon Mass the following day and remained for lunch. Marie who normally delighted in having someone at table with a more demanding palate than the pastor's seemed uncharacteristically cool, so much so that Phil noticed and called her on it.

"I'm sure you know what you're doing, Captain Keegan."

"That is a very broad statement, Mrs. Murkin, since we're being so formal."

She had been heading for the kitchen but turned in the doorway. "Why couldn't you arrest one of the others if you had to do something, the nephew or the daughter? Oh, no. It has to be someone else. Why do you always go for the little man?''

"The little man!" Keegan laughed. "I hope you don't mean Bruno Armschlager."

"You know I do."

"Then you haven't seen him. He weighs as much as I do and is half my size. And what there is of him is all muscle. Including between his ears."

"Dumb enough to be arrested?"

"Marie, we brought him in for questioning. The account in the paper was inaccurate, as usual. He was released yesterday. And you'll be happy to know that we are giving equal attention to the other heirs."

"Honestly, I don't know what things are coming to. Corpses on the steps in the morning! What next?"

"There has only been one corpse," Father Dowling said gently. He did not like to see these old friends quarreling.

"One is far more than enough."

It was difficult to argue with that, and no one was disposed to. Marie went into her kitchen on what she regarded as a note of triumph.

"So you're bringing Emily and Regis in for questioning?" Roger Dowling said.

"The missing identification of Fielding Potter showed up."

"Where was it found?"

"We got a call. Anonymous. Advising us to check Regis Potter's locker at the athletic club. That was yesterday. Not high on our list of things to do, but by gosh, there was a paper bag with a wallet, keys, handkerchief, pen, pencil, and change. The contents of his pockets, apparently."

"What is Regis's explanation?"

Phil looked at his watch. "I will know that in approximately one hour. He will stop by my office at two."

Not exactly the way Bruno had been treated, but Roger Dowling made no comment. Bruno, in any case, was indeed free and without the need of bail.

"Gone back to Miss Emily?"

"I suppose."

But at that very moment, Bruno was waiting in the front parlor, where Marie Murkin had put him. He had not had to convince her that he wanted to see the pastor alone. Would she deliver him once more into the hands of his enemy? Not that her sense of solidarity was unstrained when she saw Bruno Armschlager in the flesh.

"When I was a girl we passed around a medicine ball in physical education. That is what he looks like. A medicine ball."

It was only after Phil left that Marie told him of his visitor, and he went immediately to the parlor. Bruno sat on the edge of a chair, cracking his knuckles, nervous as a cat. If this man were ever put in jail he would lose his mind within a week, the priest decided. He put out his hand, and when it was enclosed in the vise-like grip, he wished he hadn't.

"I want to give you the money," Bruno announced.

The sudden prospect of between twenty and thirty million dollars descending on the parish of St. Hilary was one difficult to brush aside, and Roger Dowling confessed later that in a split second a new church, an architect's dream of a center for seniors, and a new rectory—why not?—sprang into being in his imagination. All for the good of the Church, of course, merely carrying on the important work already begun. Immediately after that split second, he felt like Our Lord being promised the kingdoms of the earth in exchange for a little devil worship.

Bruno, despite his leathery countenance, looked anything but diabolic. He might have been a cleverly disguised angel. In any case, the temptation, while intense, was momentary.

"That is nonsense, Bruno. I appreciate the thought, but there are far more demanding causes than this parish if you want to give away your money."

"I don't want the money."

"I understand that. If I were you, I would sit down with Mr. Cadbury and discuss how you might help a number of worthwhile causes. Why, you could set up the Bruno Armschlager Foundation and provide aid for many causes over many years. Mr. Cadbury would be happy to explain it to you. But we don't need money at St. Hilary's."

Did he hear a disapproving cough in the direction of the kitchen? Marie Murkin considered it a duty to keep herself informed on parish business and would have taken unkindly to any suggestion that she eavesdropped.

"I want you to have it."

This medicine ball obviously could accommodate only one idea at a time. Fielding Potter must have had a sense of humor, leaving such an amount to Bruno.

"I'll speak to Mr. Cadbury for you."

"You take it."

"Bruno, why St. Hilary's?"

Apparently he didn't understand the question. And then Roger Dowling grew bold.

"Bruno, did you put Mr. Potter's body on the school steps?"

He did not answer, but something reminiscent of a smile disturbed his mouth. It looked like a healed wound in repose and opened to reveal a very even row of lower teeth. And then he rose. Was it fanciful to take his reaction as an affirmative answer to the question? But Bruno had done all the visiting he intended to do.

At the door he said again, "You take the money." And Roger Dowling repeated, "I will speak to Mr. Cadbury for you."

And then as the masseur rolled down the walk, the priest called after him. "Austin Beatty comes here, you know. Would you like to see him?"

There was a hitch in his gait, as if he would stop, but he continued on to the van parked at the curb and in a moment drove slowly away.

Roger Dowling went out the door himself then and over to the school, where he found Austin Beatty playing bridge. At the moment, fortunately, he was dummy, and Roger motioned him away from the table.

"It was nice of you to visit Bruno Armschlager the other day."

A frown, then anger. "Bruno is an idiot."

"Because he doesn't want the money?"

"I could see the family trying to take it from him, but the idiot wants to give it back."

"He just tried to give it to me."

"Are you serious?"

"I refused, of course. I suggested that he have a lawyer set up a benevolent foundation if he wants to give it away."

Austin's face returned to its normal taciturnity.

"Not a bad idea."

"Why would Bruno bring the body of Fielding Potter here, Austin? It seems more deliberate than accidental that he should have put it on the steps of St. Hilary's school."

"You've talked with Bruno?"

"He just left."

"And he tried to give you how many millions of dollars?"

"What is your point?"

"Whatever Bruno does, and say he did put Potter's body where it was found, always makes a lot of sense."

"You may be right."

He entered the rectory by the front door, and a clearly disturbed Marie Murkin awaited him.

"I was just going to come looking for you."

"Is something wrong?"

Marie jerked her head in the direction of the study and made a series of odd faces.

"Is someone here?"

She parodied a slap. He was supposed to enter into her charades.

"Miss Potter is waiting for you in your study, Father Dowling." And Marie stamped back to the kitchen.

Emily had lifted her dark glasses to her forehead and was peering at books. She dropped her glasses before she turned.

"So much poetry. But then you read Tennyson for Father, didn't you?"

"Just the usual things."

"I do not consider Lope de Vega the usual thing."

"Please sit down."

He had invited her to come discuss her soul, and his bluff had been called. He certainly did not want the discussion to begin with poetry.

"I have something on my conscience, Father, and I must discuss it. Am I right in thinking you would accept death before revealing a confidence?"

He smiled. "That is a strong statement of it, but feel free to speak."

"My cousin Regis has been questioned because the things missing from my father's body were found in his possession."

"In his locker at the athletic club."

"That's right." It is difficult to have a conversation with someone when you cannot see their eyes. "Regis is guilty of many things, but I cannot see him accused of killing my father."

"Has that accusation been made?"

"No, but one can see the beginning of a chain. The assumption will be that he took those things from my father. Next will follow the assumption that he killed my father. He did not."

"You are very sure."

"Those items were put where they were found."

"How do you know that?"

She sat in silence for a while. "Because Bruno had them in his possession. Now you see why I wanted this to be confidential."

"No. I don't."

"Because I don't want Bruno accused of murdering my father any more than I want Regis to be."

"But, Miss Potter..."

"Emily."

"Emily, you yourself said it. The one who had those things could very well be the one who killed your father."

"You don't know Bruno."

"I don't know Regis either, not well enough to make such a judgment. Emily, your father was killed. Someone did it. Someone left him on the steps of the school here."

"That is what puzzles me. None of us knew you before these events. Do you suppose that everything that happened was meant to bring us all together?"

"Not for a minute." He turned toward the window and caught a glimpse of Austin Beatty lunging for the shuttlecock in a game in progress behind the school.

"It has had that effect."

"Emily, do you know a man named Austin Beatty?"

She sat back abruptly. "Do you know everyone and everything?"

"Then you do?"

"He was one of my father's most valuable employees. For years. He often said that some significant fraction of his success was due to Mr. Beatty."

"Did they part amicably?"

"Oh, Father threw a magnificent banquet. Even I was forced to go, who had never met Austin Beatty before in my life, though I had been hearing his praises sung for years. Speeches, champagne, a great fete."

"A gold watch?"

"Everything. Including the complete works of John D. MacDonald, leather bound, his favorite author."

"I don't think I know him."

"And that was the only time I ever saw Austin Beatty."

"You can see him again from that window."

"Really."

"Better still, we can go over to the school, and you can meet him."

"Whatever for? But tell me, what am I to do about Regis?"

"I have a revolutionary suggestion. Why not tell the police what you know?"

"And jeopardize Bruno?"

"Nothing will happen to Bruno."

"You seem very sure of that."

"I am," Father Dowling said, and he did not sound happy saying it. "Bruno did not kill your father."

AT FIRST, when the senior center was new, Edna Hospers let people stay until they left, which usually meant until a son or daughter came to pick them up. But it had proved wise to fix 5:30 as closing time, and at 5:20 Roger Dowling went once more from rectory to school. Not everyone stayed until 5:30, and he did not want to miss Austin Beatty.

And he didn't. Austin stood on the stairs where the body of Fielding Potter had been found, lighting a cigarette with cupped hands as if a strong wind was blowing.

"We are part of a dwindling fraternity, Austin," the priest said, indicating his pipe.

Austin squinted through smoke. "Do people nag even priests about tobacco?"

"I tell them the only nonsmoking area I aspire to is in the next world."

"And they tell you you'll get there quicker if you smoke in this one."

The two men started walking across the playground. There had been no need to mention to Beatty that he wished to speak with him. Had he expected this?

"Are you having second thoughts about Bruno's offer, Father Dowling?"

"Not about accepting it, no."

"How so then?"

"I've been wondering why Fielding Potter didn't mention you in his will."

"Me?" He had been lifting his cigarette to his lips, and the remark caused only the slightest hitch in the movement.

"Emily Potter told me how grateful her father was for all you had done for him."

"Oh, very grateful. He gave me a banquet."

It was difficult to decipher his tone of voice, except that it was very much under control.

"Emily said even she went to that."

"I remember."

"It doesn't seem much compared with twenty or thirty million dollars."

They had reached the far end of the playground, where it abutted on an empty lot in which weeds grew high and luxuriantly. Austin started down the path kids had made through the growth, but Father Dowling stopped. Six feet into the field, Austin turned.

"Let's keep walking, Father."

"Fine. But not through there."

Austin shrugged and returned to the priest. When he reached him, he abruptly grabbed Roger Dowling's arm and began to pull him down the path. His effort was unnecessary as the priest offered no resistance. When they were out of sight, Austin turned and his hitherto calm face was distorted with rage.

"So Bruno told you everything!"

"I would rather hear your version. You needn't grip my arm, Austin."

"It's why he brought the body of that old penny pincher here. The idiot thought everyone would see the connection."

"With you?"

He ignored the question as an interruption. "I had heard he meant to leave money to Bruno. To Bruno! That ape did nothing but encourage the thought that age could be overcome by exercise, and he is left a king's ransom. Potter was glad to tell me I had heard correctly. He cackled about it. He thought it very funny."

"So you killed him?"

"Yes, I killed him!" His grip on Roger Dowling's arm tightened. His expression was wild; his reason on holiday.

"Tell me about it."

As Roger Dowling suspected, Beatty was happy to describe his act of vengeance. Through Bruno, he had gained access to the grounds and confronted Potter in the gymnasium. The flaw in the plan was that Bruno knew who had been with the old man when he found him dead.

"That's why he left the body here."

"I'm surprised he didn't do you physical injury."

"So am I."

"What has this gained you, Austin?"

The question seemed to penetrate to his clouded mind. "Satisfaction!" he said through clenched teeth.

"But you had wanted money."

"I could have accepted not getting any, if he gave only to his family. But Bruno!"

"And Bruno doesn't want the money."

A pained look took possession of Austin's face. "He's crazy."

"But is he? What if you had been given thirty million dollars, Austin. What would you really have?"

Beatty looked bewildered now, his expression that of a man who suddenly realized the whole world was not worth the price of his soul.

"I'm going to the rectory, Austin. Come with me." Roger Dowling turned and walked toward the playground.

"Father, wait."

Austin's hand was briefly on his arm, but there was a thudding sound of someone approaching, and suddenly the hand was withdrawn and Austin cried out. The priest turned to see Austin Beatty in Bruno's bear grip, in an agony of pain, his feet high off the ground.

"I got him, Father," Bruno cried. "He won't lay a hand on you."

PHIL KEEGAN POURED OUT the rest of his beer and crushed the can in his palm.

"You're as strong as Bruno," Father Dowling said.

"How is the new physical-fitness center working out?"

"Working out is the right verb. The women take to it as readily as the men. Bruno has become a great favorite."

"As well as great benefactor."

"Yes." Roger Dowling puffed on his pipe. "Too generous."

Bruno had underwritten the transformation of the school gym into a physical-fitness center so that the seniors who gathered at the school each day could tone up their muscles and work off excess weight. He had tried to press a new church on the parish; he had wanted to raze the school and build a new senior center. But Roger Dowling hoped that with young families moving into the large houses in the parish, the school would be needed once again. As a trustee of the Bruno Armschlager Foundation, he had been able to head off Bruno's generosity.

Austin Beatty had been represented by Tuttle, but despite that he had been allowed to plead guilty to a charge of manslaughter and got off relatively easily.

He would be beyond the restorative powers of exercise when he was freed, but things could have gone worse for him. Father Dowling hoped they might go better. That was why he had relented and accepted Bruno's money for the shrine that had gone up along the pathway to the church. A granite plinth and a fine marble statue.

"Who is it?" Phil Keegan asked. "Statues all look alike to me."

"It's St. Jude Thaddeus."

Phil Keegan thought a minute. "Isn't he the patron of lost causes, Roger?"

"Yes, he is," said Father Dowling.

The Dutiful Son

A FATHER DOWLING
MYSTERY NOVELLA

ONE

WHEN ROGER DOWLING came out of the church after saying the noon Mass, he stopped to inhale the odor of lilacs that filled the air. The sun on his face, that wonderful smell, and the prospect of the lunch Mrs. Murkin would have ready for him added an animal contentedness to his spiritual peace.

"Father Dowling?"

He opened his eyes and, in the sunlight, had only the impression of a person, a silhouette. He stepped back, out of the sun.

"I didn't mean to startle you, Father. Could I talk with you?"

It was tempting to tell the man to come back in an hour. He did not like the prospect of being cheated out of a peaceful lunch. But that was temptation.

"Have you eaten lunch?"

"I attended your Mass."

"Come along. We can talk while we eat."

His name was Francis Stendall; he had come from Oakland, California, specifically to talk with Father Dowling about a most important matter. A matter, as it turned out, not wholly apt as a luncheon topic.

"I had no idea I was known in Oakland."

Stendall did not smile. Perhaps he thought Roger Dowling was serious. It seemed best not to assume a sense of humor in this short, stocky bald-headed man.

"I came to see whoever was the pastor of St. Hilary's."

Marie Murkin, reconciled to this stranger consuming half the lunch she had prepared for the pastor, began to apportion it between them.

"My parents lived in this parish many years ago."

"Stendall?" Marie said, giving it some thought. The guest looked surprised that the housekeeper should enter into the conversation.

"How long ago was that?" Roger Dowling asked.

"It was during the depression. Nineteen thirty-one, perhaps thirty-two."

"That was before your time, wasn't it, Marie?"

She glared at him and huffed off to the kitchen with a serving bowl.

"I have the address. Before coming to you, I found the house."

"I see."

"I want an exhumation."

"An exhumation?" This seemed an abrupt change of subject. Father Dowling had thought they were talking of the house in which Stendall's parents had lived.

It emerged that the two topics were one. Francis had the story from his mother, who told it to him in great detail during her final days. "She died of cancer two months ago. She exacted a promise from me, and I am here to keep it." Francis Stendall had the look of a man who did not make promises easily and kept the ones he made.

Roger Dowling was forming the somewhat grotesque idea that Stendall's mother had made her son promise to exhume her body, ship it from California, and bury it in the yard of the house in which they had lived all those years ago. Not wholly off the mark, as it turned out.

"My mother gave birth to a baby while they lived in that house. The baby died almost immediately. The doctor, who was a Catholic, baptized the baby and helped my father bury the body in the backyard." He waited for a shocked reaction from Roger Dowling, and when he did not get one, went on. "I of course was shocked by this. My first thought was that it was illegal. But that was the least of my mother's concerns. Everyone was poor then, as she told it, and burial expenses for a dead infant would have been a luxury. They buried the baby in the yard to save money."

"Is that what bothered your mother?"

"Oh no. Not at all. It was the thought of her child lying in unconsecrated ground, perhaps liable to be dug up accidentally. It weighed on her mind that new construction would have taken place, that perhaps a high-rise building had been put up over that grave site. What would then have happened to the remains? She could not be at peace until she knew her child would be exhumed and reburied in consecrated ground. I assured her it would be done."

"Well."

"I have come to you for two reasons. I would like you to be there when the digging is done. And you will know how to go about doing this."

"Well, I know whom to call anyway."

He called Phil Keegan, captain of detectives on the Fox River police force, and old friend, and after a number of other calls suggested by Phil, got in touch with McDivitt, the undertaker, as well. All problems but one were swiftly solved.

"Have you talked with the present owner?" Father Dowling asked.

"My hope is that it will be a parishioner of yours."

Roger Dowling had the feeling that he was the one keeping Stendall's promise to his mother. Well, why not?

"What is the address?"

"It's a house on Macon. 3306."

While Roger Dowling tried to visualize the neighborhood, a voice was heard from the kitchen.

"Whelans," Mrs. Murkin called. "The Whelans live there. Have for years. I don't envy you asking Jennings Whelan if you can drop by and dig a hole in his yard."

Francis Stendall cocked an ear as Marie spoke, then said to Roger Dowling, "I'm sorry. I didn't hear all that. My hearing is going, just as my father's did."

"Mrs. Murkin thinks I had better contact the present owner right away."

"Is it a parishioner?"

Fortunately Stendall did not hear the laugh from the kitchen.

Jennings Whelan had been on the books of the parish for years, but two years ago he informed Roger Dowling that he no longer recognized in the Catholic church the faith of his fathers.

"Mr. Whelan, I assure you that nothing that takes place at St. Hilary's..."

"St. Hilary's has nothing to do with it. It's been my parish, yes. But as part of a diocese, part of a global church. I used to know where the church stands. Now every paper I read seems to have some crazy nun or priest denying the creed. I give up."

It had been the start of a long and eventually unsuccessful argument. Roger Dowling had been unable to convince Whelan that, whatever he might hear on the news, there was more clarity about Catholic teaching now than there had ever been. But every time he had made headway, some other outrage would make Whelan's anger return, more virulent each time.

"This isn't personal, Father Dowling. I have nothing against you."

"Come to Mass, Jennings. Say your prayers. Don't let things upset you so."

"I'll say my prayers. Don't worry about that. But I'll support the church again when it gets its act together."

What would Jennings Whelan make of the request Father Dowling must convey to him on Stendall's behalf?

"I'll come with you," Stendall said.

"I think I'd better go alone."

"Whatever you say." He seemed relieved. "I am staying at the Holiday Inn just outside Elgin. I'll call you tonight."

He had rented a car and now drove away in it. Marie Murkin cleaned up with a little smile on her face.

"You should have taken him with you," Mrs. Murkin said.

Father Dowling decided not to give her a chance to repeat her condemnation of Jennings Whelan. The man's decision to stop coming to Mass had prompted a good old-fashioned anathema from the housekeeper.

"What if everyone did that?" she wanted to know.

"I couldn't afford to keep you on."

"Hmph. No Jennings Whelan is driving me out of here."

Now he said how admirable it was of Francis Stendall to fulfill his mother's dying wish.

"I don't wonder it bothered her. Burying a baby in the backyard. What did Captain Keegan think of that?"

"You mean rather than the front yard?"

"You know what I mean."

"They won't prosecute."

Suddenly there was a glint in her eye. "Maybe they can prosecute Jennings Whelan."

Marie didn't care what the charge or pretext; she wanted Whelan punished for failing to come to Mass.

TWO

ROGER DOWLING DECIDED to stop by Whelan's without telephoning first. This did not seem like a good idea when he stood at the Whelan door, pressing the door bell for the fourth time.

Still no answer. Roger Dowling walked around the house, and there was Whelan in a lawn chair. He wore swimming trunks and a sun hat, but his large body, white as the belly of a beached fish, was exposed to the sun.

"Mr. Whelan?"

He came sputtering awake, looked up, and tried to get to his feet. He lost his balance and began to trip across the lawn until Roger Dowling caught his arm and steadied him. His hat askew on his head, Whelan regarded the priest.

"You have me at a disadvantage, Father Dowling."

"I am truly sorry. I rang the bell several times and then took the chance of coming round to the backyard."

"I was catching some of this sun."

Roger Dowling looked out over the quarter acre of grass that made up a yard surrounded by a high hedge that provided Whelan with privacy for his sunbathing. The edges of the lawn were lined with flower beds, and there was another set halfway to the back, a circular plot alive with spring blossoms.

"I see you are quite a gardener."

"I am not. That is Imelda."

Mrs. Whelan. "She does a splendid job." Imelda Whelan slipped away to Mass without her husband knowing it.

"She wouldn't have heard the bell," Whelan explained. "She is taking a nap. As I was."

"You must forgive me."

"I hope you don't think you can change my mind about you know what."

"I never lose that hope. But that is not why I'm here."

"I watched a talk show last night, local. Some woman on it claimed she was a nun. She looked like a weight lifter. All about how terrible her life was, everyone telling her what to do just because she took the vow of obedience."

"A man whose parents once lived in this house came to see me today."

Whelan looked confused.

"His parents lived here in the early thirties."

"I bought it in forty-two," Whelan said.

"He has a most unusual request to make."

Whelan smiled indulgently. "Not unusual at all. I know just how he feels. Drove into south Chicago a few years ago and stopped at the house where I grew up. Asked if I could take a look at the inside again. Nostalgia. They let me. A colored family."

"This is more than nostalgia. In fact it isn't nostalgia at all. I don't think this man ever lived here."

"Stendall?"

"He lives in California. His mother died recently, and he promised her to exhume the body of an infant and have it reburied in consecrated ground."

Whelan looked at Father Dowling as he must look at talk shows. "I don't follow you."

"His mother had the baby in this house. It died almost immediately."

"Yes."

"They buried the baby in the yard."

"In the yard? Good God!"

"The idea is to rebury the child."

"You want to dig up the yard?"

"I'm afraid that's the idea."

"You say they buried a baby here." Whelan looked out on the carefully kept lawn, at the flower beds that ringed it. He had the air of a man whose home has just become an unfamiliar place.

"You'll have to talk to Imelda about that, Father."

Imelda had even more difficulty grasping the nature of the request than her husband. Jennings had put on clothes now and sat listening to Father Dowling explain it to Imelda. This might have been one more proof that the world was coming unglued.

"Dig up the yard? But where will they dig?"

"His mother gave him very explicit instructions, which he will pass on to McDivitt."

"The undertaker."

He kept at it, not losing his patience. After all, this was not an ordinary request. Imelda Whelan did not like the thought of her yard being dug up, but that was not the worst of it.

"You mean all these years there has been a body buried out there?"

"We've been living in a cemetery," Jennings said with mordant satisfaction. He was not a lot of help.

Eventually Imelda and then Jennings Whelan gave their permission. He had assured them that the legal aspects had been looked into and that McDivitt knew his business. Neither Whelan looked happy to be reminded of McDivitt's trade; they were all too likely to provide business for him in the near future. But perhaps what swung it was that they wanted any corpse in the backyard removed. Jennings said he didn't think he could sunbathe out there until the matter had been taken care of.

It was a somewhat weary but satisfied Roger Dowling who returned to his rectory. He said his office, read a few cantos of the *Purgatorio*—Dante was one of his two favorite authors; St. Thomas Aquinas being the other—smoked a pipe, drank coffee and was well disposed when Phil Keegan called to suggest they watch the Cubs tonight. He meant at the rectory, of course, and he was inviting himself for dinner as well. There was never an objection from Marie when Phil Keegan joined Father Dowling at table.

"Good," Marie said. "I want to ask him about this business of burying people in your backyard."

"I wouldn't advise it, Marie. This was during the depression, and unusual things were permitted then."

"You mean they asked permission?"

"Oh, I doubt that."

It must have been a sad scene, a man whose infant had not survived, out in his backyard with the doctor consigning it to the ground. How that must have haunted the parents over the years.

Francis Stendall called while Phil was there, and Roger Dowling told him that everything was set for the following day.

"So soon?"

"There's no point in delay."

"I hadn't expected it would be tomorrow, Father, I'm not sure I can be there." -

"Well, that isn't necessary, of course. The reburial won't be tomorrow in any case. There are legal delays."

"Could I call you at this time tomorrow?"

"Of course."

He and Phil talked a bit about the strange case, but the conversation wandered, both because the Cubs made an unexpected rally in the late innings and because Phil was inclined to want to pursue Jennings Whelan's grievances.

"He's right, Roger. Look at the church now and when we were kids."

"Look at us."

"The church is supposed to stay the same."

"It is supposed to last until the end of time. That's not the same as not changing."

He was glad to get off the subject when the fortunes of the game changed, and the Cubs snatched defeat from the jaws of victory.

After Phil had gone, Roger Dowling sat up in the study, having a final pipeful, thinking again of that long-ago scene: a father and the doctor digging a grave in the backyard of a home in Fox River to bury a newborn infant who had not survived. Despite the mother's fear, the infant had lain undiscovered all these years. Maybe it would have been best to let well enough alone.

THREE

McDIVITT, with the instructions he had been given by Stendall, made short work of it. Unfortunately, the digging had to be done where it disturbed a round flower bed in the middle of the lawn, and Imelda had to be persuaded again.

"Thank God you're here, Father," McDivitt whispered. Pink complexion, hair like cotton, McDivitt did not look like a man who had made a living burying the dead.

The body was found ten minutes later. But it was the body of an adult, not of a child. Also found was a valise containing stocks and bonds. McDivitt stopped the operation at once.

"The police must be called," he announced. He obviously thought he had been deceived, and he did not like it. But his surprise was nothing compared with Father Dowling's.

"I'll call them," he said.

The Whelans were in the house, preferring not to witness what was happening in the backyard.

"Are they done?"

"The police are going to have to be called."

"Doesn't McDivitt have a licence?"

"The body that has been found is that of an adult, not a child."

Imelda Whelan had not understood, and her husband repeated it to her. Her mouth fell open as if she were going to cry out, but no sound came. Perhaps the old do not need to make noise.

"Some money has been found too," Roger Dowling said, as he dialed Phil Keegan's number.

"I'd better go out there," Jennings Whelan said.

Phil arrived, and he had brought Cy Horvath and Agnes Lamb with him, as well as a mobile lab unit. The Whelans looked more and more like guests in their own home.

"Get a hold of this guy Stendall," Phil told Cy Horvath.

"He's staying at the Holiday Inn in Elgin," Roger Dowling said. "I'll call him."

"Wait," Phil said, "I want to think a minute." But in less than a minute, he said, "Call him but don't tell him what happened."

"Are they going to keep digging until they find the baby?" Jennings Whelan wanted to know.

"If there is a baby," Keegan growled.

There was no Francis Stendall registered at the Holiday Inn in Elgin. Nor had there been in recent days. It was a confused Roger Dowling who put down the phone and thought about his conversations with Stendall.

"I checked the plat book," Whelan said. "If they lived here, they were renters. No Stengels ever owned this house."

"Stendalls."

"No one with a name anything like that."

Roger Dowling went out into the backyard, where the mobile lab unit had put the body on a large rubbery sheet and was peeling back the burlap in which it was rolled. It was like seeing a mummy unwrapped.

The crew, after some preliminary examination, put the corpse in a body bag and sent it downtown. The valise went into another car. Two experts remained to examine the burial site.

"I feel like a fool," Roger Dowling said to Phil Keegan.

"He must have made up the story just to get that body dug up."

"And the stocks?"

"I'll bet he didn't know about that."

"Whoever he is."

"Don't worry, Roger. We'll find him."

Roger Dowling walked back to the rectory, wishing he could share Phil's confidence. From half a block away he saw the car parked in front of the house. His step quickened. He was certain that was the car Francis Stendall had been driving the day before.

Caution overcame him as he neared the house, and he cut through the playground of the school in order to approach the rectory from the church. This brought him to the kitchen door.

He went up the three steps to the back porch, then stopped, frozen in place. Voices. From the kitchen. Marie Murkin's and Francis Stendall's!

The voices went back and forth, antiphon and response, seemingly just an ordinary conversation, a passing back and forth of words to make the time go. After what had happened in the Whelans' backyard, Father Dowling felt no compunction at all about eavesdropping. Marie seemed to be reassuring the man.

"It's perfectly understandable," she said.

"No, it is cowardly. It's not as if it were a brother I had known."

"Were you born in Fox River?"

"No. My parents moved west before I was born."

Roger Dowling tried to detect duplicity in the man's voice but could not. What a consummate actor he was. The priest backed silently off the porch, to make another audible approach to the door, and nearly bumped into an old man. Erickson. If Erickson had not put out a hand to stop him, Roger Dowling would have toppled the ancient parishioner.

"Mr. Erickson, I'm sorry."

The old man looked warily at the pastor. Erickson had reached an age where everyone treated him like a child, an idiot child. Confused by the way Roger Dowling had come off the porch, he seemed on the verge of thinking that his mind really had gone.

"Oh, it's you," Marie said from the doorway. She meant Roger Dowling. "Hello, Mr. Erickson." Her voice changed as she addressed the old man.

"Thanks," Roger Dowling said to Erickson, in a normal voice. "I might have fallen."

"When I was a kid we used to do that, walk backward." Erickson's face, though lined, had a peaches-and-cream look about it; little wisps of white hair stood up on his head. He looked newborn.

"How did everything go?" Stendall said, coming out on the porch.

He seemed the same as he had the day before. There was no apprehension in his voice or manner, no indication that he knew what had been dug up in that yard.

"Not quite as expected."

"How do you mean?"

"Let's go inside." He turned. "Good-bye, Mr. Erickson. Thanks again. Are you going back to the school?"

A little delay and then Erickson nodded. Roger Dowling waited until he started back to the school, which had been turned into a center for senior parishioners.

"How about lemon meringue pie?" Marie said brightly. There were two plates on the kitchen table. When in Doubt, Serve Food was Marie's motto.

"We better talk in the study," Roger Dowling said to Stendall, avoiding Marie's look of disappointment. Clearly she wanted all the gory details.

Roger Dowling shut the door of the study after Stendall was seated and then went around the desk and got settled.

"I tried to call you from the Whelans' house."

"I was probably already here."

"The Holiday Inn in Elgin said you weren't staying there."

"Did I say Holiday Inn? I'm at the Howard Johnson's."

Roger Dowling opened the telephone directory to the yellow pages, found the number, and dialed it. Stendall looked puzzled. A voice said, "Howard Johnson's."

"Mr. Stendall's room, please."

"One moment."

Roger Dowling listened to the phone ring, looking across his desk at Francis Stendall.

"Why are you doing that?" Stendall said, genuinely puzzled. Roger Dowling put down the phone.

"It was not an infant who was buried in that yard. It was an adult."

Francis Stendall watched him as if waiting for a clue that the priest did not mean what he was saying. "An adult?"

"The body was wrapped in burlap sacks. A man apparently. The remains were taken away."

"My God." Francis Stendall sat back in his chair as if he had been pushed.

"Is there anything you want to change in what you have told me thus far, Mr. Stendall?"

But Stendall was staring at a bookshelf, not seeing it.

"Did your parents own that house?"

He looked at Roger Dowling, there and not there. "No. No, they rented it. They were poor."

"Do you have any idea who that man is?"

"No. Of course not."

"Your mother gave you instructions on where to dig."

"Yes, yes."

"Then she must have known what was buried there."

"She told me it was a child, her child." He looked at Roger Dowling. "Was she lying?"

That was not a question on which Roger Dowling could be of any help to the man. He lit his pipe while his visitor was clearly reviewing those moving scenes he had described the day before, his mother's death-bed, the anguished tale of the stillborn infant, extracting the promise that he would have her child exhumed and buried in consecrated ground.

"Was your mother prepared to die?"

"She knew for months it was inevitable. I used to think that would be an advantage. Now I don't know."

"In what way an advantage?"

He looked at the priest as if he should not have to explain. "You could prepare."

"Did your mother see a priest?"

He nodded slowly, as if not quite trusting his memory.

"Before or after she told you this story?"

"Both. She saw the priest frequently. Father, I still can't believe that she lied."

"What we know is that where she told you an infant was buried the body of an adult was found." He still did not want to mention the valise.

"I wonder whose body it is," Francis Stendall said.

"I should tell you that when the body was found, the police asked me to contact you. I called the Holiday Inn and you were not there. They—I—assumed your story about the infant was merely a device to have the adult body found."

"But I didn't know!"

Roger Dowling believed him now. "They will want to talk with you, I'm afraid."

"Of course." He rubbed his forehead as if it ached.

"There's something else."

"What?" He seemed ready for a further blow.

"A valise was found with the body. It contained stocks and bonds."

He actually sighed. "My parents were poor."

He almost cheered up. Whatever dark speculation had been going through his mind was eradicated by the news of the stock certificates. He pushed back his chair. "I'll go see the police now."

"Why don't we have them come here? Captain Keegan often comes to my Mass at noon. We can all have lunch together."

"I'll go to Mass too."

FOUR

THE BODY was that of a male adult of perhaps thirty years of age. It had been lying in the yard for nearly half a century. It was going to be very difficult to make an identification.

"It's more a research problem than anything," Phil said, laying into Marie's lasagna. "Checking old newspapers."

"How did the man die?" Francis Stendall asked.

"Oh, there's no difficulty there. He was shot." Phil wiped his mouth with his napkin and called to the kitchen, "Marie, this is marvelous!"

"Would you like more?"

"As long as you're up."

Francis Stendall had reached a numbed point where further information simply registered without reaction on his part.

"What about the money?"

"That should be easier."

"How much is there?" Roger Dowling asked.

"It's difficult to say. Some of the companies may be extinct, or they may have been absorbed by others. But it will amount to a large sum."

"Who does it belong to?"

Keegan shrugged. "All I know is that Whelan said he was going to talk to his lawyer. He thinks if it was found in his yard it ought to be his."

"Does he want the corpse too?"

Phil was watching Marie refill his plate. He smiled at Roger Dowling. "I'll ask him."

"More lasagna, Francis?" Marie asked their other guest.

"No. No, thanks. It's good."

"You should eat."

This nostrum held little appeal for him, and Roger Dowling felt sorry for the man. He had come on a pious mission, keeping a promise to his mother, and was caught up in a mystifying business.

Over the next several days, some things became clear. Or rather, things became more obscure when the conclusion became unavoidable that the man who had been dug up in the Whelans' backyard was Stendall's father. Roger Dowling had asked Stendall if he would like to stay in a guest room at the rectory while this baffling matter was being investigated, and he accepted with relief.

"I'll turn in my rented car too. It's costing me a fortune." As a teacher, Stendall did not have money to throw around, and Roger Dowling was happy to help him cut down on his expenses. When Phil called the rectory to reveal the startling turn of events, Stendall was upstairs reading.

"The damnedest thing, Roger. The dental records match those of a man who served in the First World War whose name was Philip Stendall."

"And he was about thirty when he died?"

"Do me a favor, Roger. Ask him what his father's name was."

"Philip," Francis Stendall answered. "Why?"

"What kind of man was he?"

"We didn't have many photographs of him, and my mother was reluctant to talk about him. I do have a diary he kept in France."

"France?"

"He was in the AEF in World War I. He was gassed and sickly, and I guess that's why he died so young. He was a delayed casualty of the war."

"Did he die in California?"

Stendall nodded. "Why all the questions?"

"Francis, there is a possibility that the buried body is that of your father."

There was no way to cushion the blow, so he didn't try. Poor Stendall had been absorbing so much psychic punishment that this added horror brought no visible reaction. His cigarette had hesitated as he brought it to his lips, but he dragged on it and then let smoke slip from his mouth.

"My father."

"Is it possible he never went to California?"

"I have only my mother's word." He smiled sadly. "I asked her where he was buried, and she said a military cemetery. That was one of the things I always wanted to do, find out where he was buried, visit his grave. The tomb of the unknown father."

He fell silent. Neither of them said anything of the fact that the body of a dead stranger was now Stendall's father. The big question remained: Who had killed him?

Stendall excused himself, saying he wanted some air, some time to think of all this. From the window, Roger Dowling watched the man pace back and forth on triangular walkway that ran between rectory, school, and church. He disappeared into the church for a time and then emerged. Roger Dowling had gone back to his desk, and when he looked out again he saw Stendall talking with Erickson. He tried to get away, but Erickson stayed with him. Finally they parted, and Stendall came inside.

"I see you met Erickson, the old fellow."

"He didn't say what his name was. That's a good idea, using the school for old people."

"It's a place for them to come."

"Are they all parishioners?"

"Mostly. We don't turn anyone away. Erickson has lived in the parish forever I guess."

"He wanted to know if I did. I said no, and he asked my name. I really must look woebegone."

"Why?"

"I had the impression he was trying to cheer me up." He sighed. "I guess there's no escaping the fact that my mother killed my father."

Roger Dowling said nothing.

"It's the only way it makes sense. The guilt she felt was real enough, but she couldn't tell me the source of it, not even when she was dying. I guess I'm not surprised. But she had made up her mind she wanted me to know what she had done."

"Why?"

"The stocks? I don't know. Where did they come from?"

That was the other clarification that did not clarify. No report of missing stocks had shown up. No robbery, no misappropriation of funds. Stendall had thought his father was an invalid, that he had received a pension until he died. But there was no record of his having been gassed or wounded in any way. He had not received a pension.

The Stendalls had had a phone, a forty-call number, as it was classified, a special low rate unless the number of their calls exceeded forty a month.

Cy Horvath paused and looked across the desk at Father Dowling. "That's the kind of thing they've filled computers with."

"Where did Stendall work?"

"He was a bank guard."

Roger Dowling's brows lifted. "Is that where the money came from?"

Horvath shook his head. "There is still no indication on that. We've got people inheriting money, that sort of thing, but no big theft. Twenty-five dollars would have counted as a major haul in the early thirties."

Who would get it? Jennings Whelan called to ask Father Dowling to stop by. An urgent matter. Dowling went over, wondering if the odd events of recent days had prompted a change of heart in Whelan, but the urgent matter did not concern the recalcitrant parishioner's soul.

"Imelda is mad as blazes because I say that money is ours. Can you imagine that?"

"Mr. Whelan, right now I can imagine almost anything."

"Would you talk with her?"

"To what purpose?"

"Talk some sense into her."

"You mean, persuade her you should initiate lengthy, costly legal proceedings of dubious outcome?"

Whelan threw back his shoulders. "You've been talking with Amos Cadbury."

"Is he your lawyer?"

"Not on this matter! He doesn't think the court would go my way, necessarily. Do you know why?"

Roger Dowling shook his head. "I haven't discussed it with Amos."

"I'll tell you why. Because I'm not an heir or consign of the poor devil they dug up. Does he think they're going to find a relative when they don't know who he is?"

"They've identified him, Mr. Whelan. And he does have an heir."

Whelan's face went blank and he sat down. "You're not just saying that?"

Imelda Whelan, who must have been listening from another room, came and put her arm about her husband.

"Who was he, Father?"

"A man named Stendall."

"No. I meant the corpse."

"That's what I mean. It appears that the body is that of the father of the man who asked it to be dug up."

"Telling us it was a baby!" Whelan shook his head at the baseness of mankind. "He knew it was his father, and he knew there was money."

"How did he die?" Imelda asked.

"He was shot."

"Killed himself and tried to take it with him?" But even Whelan saw the silliness of that remark. He said, "I have been assuming they wouldn't be able to identify him."

Imelda patted her husband's shoulder. The remark was equivalent to a statement of a complete change of heart. He was going to reject his dreams of avarice.

FIVE

AMOS CADBURY was more than willing to represent
Francis Stendall in any claim he wished to make for
the money. "If it isn't stolen and it was found with
him and the man is his son, I should think the decision would go in his favor. Of course there will be
taxes. And my fee. Both exorbitant, needless to say."
Amos paused. The silence indicated he had made a
joke. "That will still leave a considerable sum."

"I will suggest that he contact you."

But Francis Stendall shook his head. "No, Father.
I don't want it. I don't know where it came from or
how it got into the grave with him, but it doesn't interest me."

"You might want to think about it more before you
decide."

"I won't change my mind. It would be ghoulish.
Do you know what I thought of when you first mentioned the money? *Treasure Island.* I would bet there
is some story of greed and treachery that explains the
money. Dear God, I wish my mother were still alive
so I could ask her some questions. Why did she want
to put me through this?"

"When you first talked to me it was with the intention of reburying an infant in consecrated ground."

He nodded. "Of course. Could we do that for my father?"

"Certainly."

"A funeral Mass too?" He shook his head. "After all these years I'll be able to attend my father's funeral. And only weeks after attending my mother's."

"Maybe that is what she really wanted, not to put you through an agonizing experience."

"She should have told me."

"It is not easy for us to admit to having done something so wrong."

"Murder?"

"We don't know that."

"That is what is hard. Not knowing."

AGNES LAMB CONTINUED the routine search, trying to locate anyone who had been a neighbor of the Stendalls' all those years ago. And she came up with two people, a man and a woman, unrelated, who had lived as children in the neighborhood. They were both in their sixties and, somewhat to Agnes's surprise, seemed to consider it perfectly normal to be asked about a neighborhood as it had been well over half a century ago.

"They talk about it as if nothing had changed. The man, Peters, can close his eyes and name every family on the block, both sides of the street. Of course he still lives there.''

''In the same house?''

''When he married he brought his wife home and they stayed there when his parents died. The woman's memory is much more selective.''

''How so?'' Roger Dowling noticed that Keegan looked on with approval as the black officer showed how good she was. He had come downtown to Phil's office to hear what Agnes had found.

''She remembers her mother talking about the Stendalls. One or the other was being unfaithful; she doesn't remember which, if she ever did know. Anyway, the move to California was meant to solve that problem.''

''Remove one or the other from temptation?''

''That's right. Rose says her mother always thought it was someone who lived right there on the block.''

''Well, well.''

Phil said, ''Tell him your theory, Agnes.''

She made a little bow. ''I say he was the one fooling around and that mama put him in the cold cold ground. The California move was meant to cover that. Or maybe they decided to go, and he started acting up again, a last fling.''

''Why the money?'' Roger Dowling asked.

''That is the flaw in the ointment, Father,'' Agnes said. ''But I don't know any theory that's going to make burying that much money and just leaving it there make much sense.''

"Maybe leaving it there wasn't part of the plan."

"Well, then the plan fell through."

Of course it could have been buried by mistake, but such explanations were considered the last refuge of the scoundrel in Phil Keegan's department. He urged his people to live in a completely determined universe; every event had a cause. It was just that sometimes they weren't able to find it. But that is what they must believe, not that something just *happened* one way as opposed to a million others.

Agnes handed him a print-out of her findings. They were counting on him to keep Stendall informed, figuring he had a right to know whatever they learned. But how much more bad news about his parents could the poor fellow take?

On the way back to St. Hilary's, Roger Dowling decided that the remarks by the woman Agnes called Rose could be regarded as mere gossip and there was no need to pass it on to Francis Stendall. If something further came to light, maybe, but for the nonce he would not add further to Stendall's load.

THE MEMORIAL MASS and burial service for Stendall *père* went off with some pomp and circumstance. Marie urged the stalwarts of the parish to be there; Mrs. Hospers suggested to the oldsters at the school that they might want to attend, and Erickson of all people volunteered to line them up and march them over.

It was difficult to know whether Erickson knew anything about Stendall's situation, but he at least guessed the younger man had received bad news of some kind and required moral support. More than once Roger Dowling looked out to see Stendall and Erickson pacing back and forth on the parish sidewalks.

"What does he say?" Roger Dowling asked, curious.

Stendall laughed. "He doesn't get a chance to say much. I have to keep reminding myself to put questions to him. So far I've told him a lot about Mother. There isn't much I want to say about my father just now."

"I hope you haven't decided we know how your father died."

Stendall started to say something, then stopped. "Oh, it doesn't matter. I talk about growing up in California. I guess I'm looking for clues in those years for what is coming to light now. My mother was a good woman, Father. As you say, we don't know how my father died, but the fact remains that she was a good mother to me."

Aside from a few lies and deceptions. Well, Erickson might be an ideal sounding board for a man who was trying to salvage as much of his past as he could.

MERLIN OF THE *Fox River Tribune* got wind of what had been happening and wanted to interview Stendall.

"Why are you calling me?" Roger Dowling said, crossing his fingers.

"Peanuts Pianone says Stendall's been staying with you. Is that right?"

"He has been through a lot, Merlin. I really don't think he should be put through any more. Whatever story there is is over half a century old."

"That's the story!"

"Are things that slow?"

"Father, I understand what you're saying. Reacting just personally, I might feel exactly the way you do. But I have a duty to my readers. And those readers have a right to know."

A right to know what Merlin and others like him decided people should know. "Why don't you talk with Mr. Stendall about it?"

"That's why I'm calling."

"He is out of the house at the moment. Where should he call you?"

"I'll call him," Merlin said, his voice heavy with skepticism. But Stendall had left the house, if only to go over to the school and give Edna Hospers a hand. "It occurred to me that most of them are the age of my parents. The men are the age my father would have been."

It was remembering that remark that led Roger Dowling reluctantly to pick up the phone and call Phil Keegan.

"Phil, did Agnes check on births during those years?"

"Whose?"

"Was Stendall born here or in California?"

"Does it make a difference?"

"I'm just curious."

"What was he told?"

"California."

"He must have a birth certificate."

"Would you ask Agnes and have her call me?"

"What are policemen for? What did he think of the story Agnes dug up about his parents?"

"I didn't tell him. How do we know it's true?"

"Maybe you're right."

AGNES DROPPED BY a Xerox copy of the birth announcements, and Roger Dowling read that a son had been born to the Stendalls of 3306 Macon Street on April 20 at home. Perhaps being born at home was not all that unusual at the time, but the memory of Stendall's original story when he came to the rectory gave the priest an odd feeling.

He put the xeroxed page in his desk drawer, along with the papers Agnes had given him a few days before.

"Jennings Whelan is here." Marie Murkin whispered this, stagily, as she stood in the door of his study.

"Show him in."

"Not here in the rectory." She gave him a look. "At the school. With the other old people. Maybe it's a first step."

And maybe not. Should he drop by the school and accidentally run into Whelan? A tempting idea, but first he wanted to have a talk with his houseguest. Francis Stendall had said the night before he would be heading back to California soon. He hadn't done what he had come to do, but no doubt he had accomplished what his mother had in mind when she gave him those instructions. He had stood at his father's new grave the previous day, a lonely figure, staring down at the rather sumptuous casket that contained what was left of his father after more than half a century mouldering in the backyard of the house on Macon Street. To think of a man Stendall's age as an orphan is odd—who isn't an orphan when he nears sixty?—but he had the look of a man who had been abandoned by both his parents. No wonder he wanted to go back to his own life now and escape the haunting presence of his mother and father. But Roger Dowling thought he should stay on at least for a few days more.

"What's the point, Father? I feel like a parasite as it is, camping in your rectory."

"Nonsense, Marie appreciates someone with a better appetite than I have."

"I can't understand why you're not overweight. She is a wonderful cook."

And so she was. He had decided early in his tenure as pastor that he would have to hide behind the excuse of an inadequate appetite or he would balloon up like a monsignor.

"They sent over the notice of your birth in the local paper if you'd like to see it."

He shook his head. "That's one thing I am sure of, that I was born."

Roger Dowling did not push the matter. But it was agreed that Stendall would stay several more days at least.

"It sounds morbid, but if I do stay, I'd like to see that house."

"The Whelans'? I'll see if I can arrange it."

Equipped with an excuse, Roger Dowling sauntered over to the school. He dropped by Mrs. Hospers's office, and they talked a bit about the program she had developed. What he liked about it was that it left the old people to figure out many of the activities themselves. How awful it would be to fall into the hands of some breathless enthusiast who would insist they must keep busy, do this and that, whatever their inclinations.

When he went to what had been the auditorium, there were card games in process, three checkers matches, one game of chess, and of course shuffleboard. The one game all the old people seemed to like was shuffleboard. And there indeed was Jennings Whelan, playing a game with Erickson. Roger Dowling stopped at a checkers game not far from the shuffleboard area, kibitzing a while, giving Whelan a chance to notice him and disappear if he liked. But the game continued, and Roger Dowling went over just as Erickson, with a practised push, managed to remove all Whelan's markers from the target area.

"Damn it!" shouted Whelan and turned to Roger Dowling. "Did you see what that burglar did?"

"It's part of the game," Erickson said, clearly enjoying himself.

"I was counting on beginner's luck," Whelan moaned as they trudged to the other end of the playing area.

It soon became clear to Whelan that he was no match for Erickson, and he returned his pole to the rack.

"I'm going to quit while I still have my house."

"Speaking of which," Roger Dowling said, and Whelan's eyebrows went up.

"Oh, no. Not another archaeological dig in my backyard."

"Only metaphorically. Young Stendall wondered if you'd let him come visit the house."

"Why not? He managed to get the backyard ruined. He never did see the result of that, did he? Sure, send him over."

"When would be a good time?"

"Well, Carl and I are moseying back home now. He can come along now, if he wants."

"Carl's going too?"

"To his own house, of course. He's given up trying to buy mine."

"You're neighbors?"

"For my sins," Whelan said. "For my sins."

"We must talk about those some day."

"You never quit, do you, Father? You're as bad as Imelda."

"Thank God for Imelda."

Whelan puffed out his lips, then nodded vigorously. "I do. I do. The very words that got me into it, and I'd do it again tomorrow. I'm not sure she would though. Being married to a lapsed Catholic is hard on her."

"It's harder on you."

"Where is this young Stendall? We've got to get going. Right, Carl?"

"I think I'll stay," Erickson said. "You have someone to walk with now. You don't need me."

"Were you just going to do me a favor?"

Erickson didn't answer.

SIX

AFTER STENDALL AND WHELAN had gone, Roger Dowling sat at the desk in his study, smoking his pipe, looking straight ahead but not seeing anything.

After a few minutes, he opened the drawer of his desk and took out the first papers Agnes Lamb had given him. The list of residents of Macon Street when Stendall's parents had lived there. Was he really surprised to find the name of Carl Erickson on the list? And what did it mean? One thing it explained was Erickson's interest in Francis Stendall. He had known his parents, though apparently he had not admitted this to Agnes Lamb. Might he even have seen Francis as an infant? Not impossible. But Roger Dowling had the feeling that there was more.

He called Mrs. Hospers. "Edna, would you ask Carl Erickson if he would like to join me for lunch? After the noon Mass. Tell him I would particularly like him to come."

One of the advantages of saying Mass facing the people—a change that had followed on Vatican II— was that he knew who was in church. Carl Erickson was not there, and he wondered if he would show up for lunch.

"You have a guest," Marie Murkin said when he came in the kitchen door. Another answered prayer. "He's in the study."

"How glad I am you could come," Roger Dowling said when he joined Erickson.

"I don't have that busy a schedule, Father. Not anymore."

"Lucky man. Come, let's have our lunch."

Where had he gotten the impression that Carl Erickson was a doddering old imbecile? He was an enjoyable table companion, with many amusing observations about growing old, and much praise for what Mrs. Hospers was doing in the school.

"I was surprised to see Jennings Whelan here this morning," Father Dowling said.

"I suggested he come."

"Are you friends?"

"I think of him as one of the new boys on the block."

"Ah, the block. I want to talk with you about that. When we go back to the study."

"I noticed you have a complete set of St. Augustine."

"Oh, yes. I've been reading him for years."

"I know only the *Confessions*."

"Have you read it?"

"It has become a favorite. A good book for old sinners."

When they had adjourned to the study, it was easy to continue the conversation along those lines. "You seem struck by the story of Francis Stendall."

For the first time, Erickson seemed ill at ease. "It is a fairly incredible happening."

"Did you know his parents?"

There are gestures, looks, remarks that prove to be the open sesames, and that question sufficed to open Erickson's heart.

"I had wondered if that would become known. The police called and asked about the Stendalls—they knew I had lived on the block in those days—and I am afraid I lied to them. But in many ways I have been living a lie for all these years."

Roger Dowling knew that all he need do was wait, be silent, be receptive, and the story would be told.

And what a story it was. Carl Erickson had been Mrs. Stendall's lover. He used that term, not without irony. "That makes it sound much more romantic than it was. Those were gray days, Father. Impoverished days. A movie was an event. Her husband worked nights as a bank guard; my wife was tending to her sister's children. I asked Rosemary to go to the movie. It was one of those frothy depression pictures. They plied us with tales of the idle rich at a time when a square meal was rare for many. That is how it started."

It ended with Rosemary getting pregnant. Her husband was upset. He lived almost like a monk just so she wouldn't have children, not yet, and here she was pregnant.

"Both Rosemary and I formed the idea that the child was mine."

"Was it?"

Erickson looked at Roger Dowling in anguish. "I don't know. She didn't know. There was no way of knowing for sure. But she said she was sure. The child was mine. I felt as much terror as joy. I had a wife; Rosemary had a husband. It was an impossible situation. And they quarreled constantly about her pregnancy. He decided they would move to California. Like so many others he had the notion you could live in California on nothing. There was sun; there was fruit. It sounded like paradise. She thought it a crazy idea. We decided to run away. I had no money, but I had lots of worthless stock as it then was, but stock in which I never lost hope. I put all the certificates in a valise; they would go with us. Other bags were packed and waiting. I was ready to desert my wife." He said this as if even now after all these years he could not believe his intended perfidy. "But I had already been unfaithful. I seemed caught up in something that deprived me of my freedom."

And then came an awful night, a weekend when her husband was home, just days before the planned flight. They argued and she told him her child was not his. He became enraged. "She telephoned me and I went over."

He paused. "There are moments in life when everything is settled. They do not announce themselves as so significant, but in the event they are the great hinges on which everything turns.

"When I showed up, not knowing what she had told him, he immediately drew the appropriate inference. He lunged at me. We fought. He was much stronger than I. I thought he would kill me until there was a shot. She had killed him with his own revolver."

The dead body of the husband had purged them both. Any thought of running away together was now repugnant. It was one thing to be joined by a child, but to have a killing link them was too much. And so they had decided to do what they had done. In the still of the night, when there was no moon, Erickson dug the grave. Meanwhile, she got gunny sacks from the basement and wrapped him. "She seemed to want to make him warm." And then Erickson carried him out into the backyard and buried him. Before he covered the body, in a fit of disgust, as a symbol that he was rejecting his plan to flee, he pitched the valise into the grave and covered it and the body.

"I could hardly believe afterward what labor I had engaged in. Yet I did it swiftly and effortlessly, carried along by panic. When I was done, we decided she would say her husband had left for California. She would follow after her baby was born. I would let it be known that they had impetuously decided to put his romantic plan into effect."

After she left, there was complete silence. She did not write. Erickson did not know where she was or even if she had actually gone to California.

"The house was sold, then sold again to Jennings Whelan, and from time to time I would dread that the body would somehow be discovered. But I had dug deep, at least six feet, that seemed important, and there was little danger."

"Whelan said you tried to buy the house."

Erickson looked away. "I was motivated by greed rather than fear. Those worthless stocks are far from worthless now. The companies revived; shares split and split again. I do not dare guess what they are worth. I used to dream of ways of digging up that valise, but nothing feasible ever occurred to me. And then a year ago I heard from Rosemary."

He held his hands in a praying position and brought the tips of his fingers to his lips.

"She was dying. She was determined to tell her son what had happened."

"She wrote you?"

"Yes, and I telephoned her, many times. Her voice sounded unchanged, and it was like talking to the half-hysterical woman I had parted from that awful night. I begged her to keep the secret. What difference did it all make now? Her answer was that her conscience bothered her. Not the murder, she had long since confessed that, but the thought of him lying there wrapped in gunny sacks in unconsecrated ground. I was still trying to dissuade her when she died. You can imagine what it has been like for me during these past days."

Roger Dowling let silence settle, a not uncomfortable silence. It was clear that Erickson was relieved finally to have told what had happened.

Roger Dowling said softly, "I doubt very much that anyone will guess what happened."

"But you must tell the police?"

The priest shook his head. "No. I don't think so. If a crime was committed, it was not by you. Unless the burial was a crime, and that has been rectified now."

SEVEN

AFTER FRANCIS STENDALL had left for California, his strange visit over, Father Dowling missed him. Even Marie lamented not having another mouth to feed. Amos Cadbury had convinced Stendall not to disclaim the stocks until he had given it more thought.

"I won't change my mind," Stendall told Roger Dowling.

"You can give it to charity. Think of something you would like to support."

"Thank you for your hospitality, Father."

Erickson drove Stendall to the airport with who knew what emotions. Was he saying farewell to a son or not? Phil Keegan had problems of his own.

"I hate a crime where there is no criminal to indict," Phil said. It was received opinion that the wife had killed the husband.

"Well, no one profited from the crime anyway."

"I would like to know why that valise was buried with the body, Roger. There must be a perfectly logical explanation of that."

"Remorse?"

Phil laughed. It seemed to cheer him up. Marie, drawn by the laughter, brought Phil a beer, and they settled down to watch the Cubs. Perhaps there was a logical explanation of that too, but Roger Dowling did not know it.

The DOWN HOME *Heifer Heist*

Eve K. SANDSTROM

First Time in Paperback

A Sam & Nicky Titus Mystery

THIN ICE

Rancher Joe Pilkington, neighbor to Sheriff Sam Titus and photographer wife Nicky, is run down when he interrupts rustlers during a heist. Aside from tire tracks in the snow, the only clue is the sound of Mozart heard playing from the killer's truck.

Two more grisly deaths follow, and it looks as if a beloved member of the Titus ranch may be accused of murder. Sam and Nicky grimly set out to corner a killer...before they become victims themselves.

"Sandstrom makes the most of her setting...."
—*Publishers Weekly*

Available in October at your favorite retail stores.

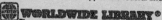

DESERT SINNER

RALPH McINERNY

A Father Dowling Mystery

TRUE CONFESSIONS
The Wilson case was delightful fare for the gossip-addicted—a Vegas showgirl lucks out and marries an impossibly rich aging playboy, takes out a large insurance policy...then kills him.

Lots of people are intrigued by Stacey Wilson, her crime and her confession, including Father Roger Dowling. And why is that handsome young man calculatedly wooing police captain Phil Keegan's love-struck secretary? Is it as innocent as it seems?

Father Dowling believes that Stacey Wilson was wrongfully convicted. And that what lies beneath the surface of an open-and-shut case will prove deadly....

"McInerny builds superb psychological portraits...."
—*Chicago Sun Times*

Available in December at your favorite retail stores.

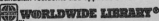

JUDAS PRIEST
RALPH McINERNY
A Father Dowling Mystery

First Time in Paperback

HIGH PRIEST OF SIN

Chris Bourke has abandoned his vocation, married a former nun and made a career out of attacking the church. His Enlightened Hedonism movement called for untrammeled pursuit of sensual pleasures—and his following was, not surprisingly, enormous.

But what does a professional apostate do when his only child announces she is going to enter a convent? He asks Father Roger Dowling for help.

Not in the business of turning away those with the call, Father Dowling agrees to speak to Sonya. But her brutal murder involves the venerable priest in a sordid tale of duplicity and deadly intent...and a clever killer with a calling of his own.

"Characterizations are excellent...."

—*Chicago Tribune*

Available in November at your favorite retail stores.

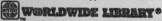